Heroes of Centerville

A Journey of Truth, Love and Transformation

John Russell

HojoPress Publications

To my daughter Breanna, who continues to inspire me to tell stories
that matter
I love you very much

Preface

In the heart of Centerpointe, a ranching town nestled beneath the wide-open skies of California, a tale unfolds—a tale of truth and transparency, friendship and solidarity, and the remarkable transformation of ordinary women into the unsung heroes of their community.

"The Heroes of Centerville" is a narrative that transcends the boundaries of fiction, for it is inspired by the untold stories of those who dare to uncover the veiled secrets that hide within the fabric of society. This book beckons you to step into the lives of women who, with unwavering resolve, challenge the status quo, revealing the profound power of truth and transparency.

At its core, this narrative pays homage to the incredible strength of friendship and solidarity. Breanna, Holli, Rebeccah, Samantha, and many others find themselves bound by a common purpose—to unveil the injustices that threaten their town. Through countless trials and tribulations, they discover that it is in unity that their true strength lies, and it is in friendship that their courage is kindled.

As you embark on this journey, let these themes remind you of the transformative potential within each of us. Let them serve as a testament to the fact that even in the unlikeliest of places, heroes can emerge. In the quiet, ranching town of Centerville, where cattle graze, and the horizon stretches endlessly, a new kind of hero is born—one who champions truth, embraces transparency and stands unwaveringly by the side of her friends.

"The Heroes of Centerville" is a tribute to the resilience of the human spirit, a celebration of the bonds that can be forged in the face of adversity, and a reminder that, indeed, women can be the unsung heroes of their own stories.

Contents

Chapter 1

The soft morning sunlight filtered through the curtains, casting a warm and gentle glow across the room. I blinked, the remnants of sleep giving way to a new day. I stretched beneath the comfort of my sheets, the air fresh and invigorating, with a hint of dew.

Centerville, California, welcomed me with a quiet serenity, unlike any place I lived before. It had a gentle breeze, swaying tall trees and flowers that lined the medians of the roads. The town had silhouettes of neighboring houses, each with families and their own stories. I was ready to bring them the daily news promising a day of possibilities.

My decision to move to Centerville was a turning point in my life. After years of relentless investigative journalism, I yearned for a change. Centerville enchanted me unexpectedly with its small-town warmth and companionship. Unlike the hectic city life, its charm and tight-knit community drew me in.

Swinging my legs out of the bed, my feet met the cool hardwood floor, sending a gentle shiver up my spine. There was a rush of energy as my auburn hair flowed around my shoulders in waves. The hue caught the light, creating a warm halo to dance with every step.

My brown eyes were deep and determined, always seeking the hidden truths beneath the surface. The scent of brewed tea wafted in from the kitchen. The comforting aroma eased any residual grogginess. It mingled with cardboard and packing tape, a reminder that boxes were still waiting to go through.

I walked across the room, opened the window, and let in the crisp morning air. A gentle breeze danced through the room, ruffling the curtains.

Each container held a piece of my past —a collection of memories and possessions that would soon be put away. The sight filled me with purpose—a reminder this was a fresh start, a chance to create a unique apartment.

While beginning to unpack, the room transformed into a sea of cardboard. Dishes were placed with a soft clink, books thudded against shelves, and linens rustled as they spread over the bed.

I unwrapped the well-padded box that held the precious treasure—a gleaming Emmy Award was a proof of my years of hard work and dedication.

A sense of pride swelled within me as I held the Emmy in my hands. I looked at the plate on the award- Breanna Willis. I was young to win the award at 32, but it was a story near and dear to my heart. The memory of the pivotal investigation at KBNW played like a filmstrip in my mind; the relentless pursuit of uncovering the story of Jeff Paulson and the web of kickbacks he orchestrated during his tenure as CEO of EthicalEdge Solutions, the late nights spent poring over documents, the interviews with insiders, and the heart-pounding moments of unveiling the shocking truth, flooded back. A sense of accomplishment that words alone couldn't capture.

I placed the Emmy on a shelf with all the honor and recognition it brought me. It once again reminded me of journalism's power to uncover injustice and spark change.

I reached for a framed photograph nestled among the unpacked items. A snapshot captured during the celebratory BBQ posts the triumphant broadcast of the Jeff Paulson & William Donavan inquiry. I stood alongside my dear friends Holli, Rebeccah, and Samantha in the photo. Broad smiles and eyes alight.

We unraveled the intricate web of the kickback scheme. Each friend brought a unique strength to the table, a vital puzzle piece. Their unwavering support and willingness to dive into the depths of the investigation filled me with a profound sense of unity and purpose.

These women had been my pillars of support, my confidantes through the challenges and victories. The laughter, the late-night discussions, and the unwavering encouragement were all encapsulated in a single frame. A tangible reminder echoing that solitude should never tread on this journey. The celebrated success mirrored the ties woven and the fortitude of our friendship.

Tracing my fingers over the photograph's glass, I couldn't help but smile. The joys of shared dreams and unbreakable connections we built over the year were a treasure far more valuable than any award.

The move to Centerville had been a leap of faith, I embraced the challenge of weaving my story into the fabric of a new community. Centerville's quaint streets and rich history welcomed me with open arms, and each encountered a brushstroke, adding depth to the canvas of my experiences. The town was a fresh start where I could carve out a new chapter in my narrative.

The Emmy symbolized triumph, recognition of my dedication, and sleepless nights. Its golden glow illuminated new paths. The station in Centerville extended an invitation to become the morning anchor. It was the beginning of my aspirations for a larger audience. My goal is to become an evening anchor.

Contemplating the weight of the position and its impact on my career—a whisper played at the edges of my thoughts. Amidst my professional considerations, an urge to delve into unexplored territories began to crystallize—an eagerness to weave myself into the unknown fabric of this new town. The windows framing my surroundings hinted at untold stories, their silent invitation pulling me beyond the threshold.

A flyer for the Farmers Market in downtown Centerville caught my eye. The idea of attending beckoned like an irresistible call. An opportunity presented itself to immerse in the rhythm of everyday existence. The booths, teeming with fresh produce and artisanal crafts, symbolized sustenance for the body and inspiration for the soul. An opportunity to connect, learn, and contribute my brushstrokes to Centerville's unfolding narrative. The event stood as an unmissable opportunity.

I set the boxes aside, ready to venture beyond my doorstep into the world outside. I was engulfed in a whirlwind of sensations.

Opting to drive to the farmer's market, I embraced the refreshing chill in the air and the sun's warmth on my skin. With the day's promising adventure, I set off from the parking lot of my apartment and down through the town. The journey was brief, and I found myself humming along to my favorite tune on the radio. Before I knew it, I had arrived at the bustling market. Stepping out of the car, I eagerly ventured towards the market entrance.

Colorful produce stalls, artisans crafting their wares, and people from all occupations converged in a lively activity dance. It greeted me with a sensory explosion dancing around. Colorful banners and handmade signs adorned the entrance, each heralding hidden treasures. The chatter of vendors and patrons filled the air, creating an atmosphere of energy and anticipation.

A cacophony of colors and textures serenaded my senses. Vibrant fruits and vegetables created a veritable rainbow, each hue more luscious than the last. The community's skill and creativity shone through in the handcrafted crafts and artisanal products, adding authenticity to the tapestry.

I saw a young couple, their faces illuminating their shared love, with a precious bundle in their arms—a baby with eyes that sparkled like the morning sun. My heart swelled at the sight, and I couldn't resist approaching them.

"Your baby is a little angel," I smiled, genuine admiration shining.

The couple's eyes lit up, and pride radiated between them. "Thank you so much!" the mother replied, her voice warmed.

I leaned in. "What's his name?"

The mother's smile deepened. "His name is Noah."

We continued our conversation, and a sense of friendship blossomed between us. The couple introduced themselves as Anna and Lucas, a nurse and teacher. Their passion for their professions was evident as they shared their lives.

They painted a vivid picture of life in Centerville. Their words wove a tapestry of a close-knit community where neighbors knew each other by name. Anna told of the events that brought everyone together, while Lucas told tales of the bustling energy in the town's schools.

I couldn't help but be drawn to their enthusiasm. "I'm Breanna," I introduced myself. "I moved here and decided to explore the local farmers market."

"You've moved to a wonderful place," Anna said.

Their welcoming expressions mirrored my sentiments. "Welcome to Centerville," Lucas said with genuine friendliness. "If you ever need anything, don't hesitate to reach out."

"Thank you," I murmured, nodding as I went onward. A gentle warmth settled in my heart as I turned away from Lucas and Anna. Their genuine hospitality and openness left an impression. A soft smile lingered on my lips as I continued. Their kind words echoed in my mind.

Approaching one of the bustling vendor booths, I looked at a man who exuded wisdom and mystery. His passion for his profession was evident, and his face was weathered. A twinkle of intrigue gleamed in his eyes as he arranged his display of handcrafted goods.

Our eyes met, and a friendly smile tugged at the corners of his lips. Something about him felt different—a sense of authenticity drew me in. I initiated a conversation.

"Hello," he greeted me. "Looking for something today?"

Returning the smile, an immediate connection. "I am just looking. I'm new in town and thought I'd explore the farmer's market. It's quite a place."

His eyes crinkled as he nodded. "Ah, a newcomer, huh? My name is Elias Harrington. Welcome to our little community. You're in for a treat."

We chatted about the town, and a sense of trust settled. I found myself sharing my background as an investigative journalist. The man's interest was genuine, and he leaned in as if about to share a secret.

"You know," he began, lowering his voice, "there's a story circulating here. People call it a conspiracy theory, but I believe there's truth to it."

My curiosity triggered, and I leaned in closer. "A story? What kind of story?"

He cast a glance to ensure no other soul lurked within hearing distance. "It's about a cattle rancher. Folks say he's been involved in some shady dealings, kickbacks, etc. It's under the rug."

Intrigued but also cautious. "Do you have any facts to support this?"

The man's eyes held a glint of earnestness. "Some say it's a rumor, but others believe there's evidence. Hidden documents tell a different story. I've talked to people who've seen things and heard things. You know what they say about a hunch—it's worth paying attention to. Our local veterinarian has been able to dig up some information that can prove the rumors."

Listening to him, conflicting emotions surged within me. His voice carried an undeniable passion, each word brimming with unwavering conviction. It stirred the investigative impulse that propelled me through countless stories. A lingering sense of caution held me back. This path might lead me into a misinformation maze.

"You believe this story, then?" I asked, my tone measured.

He nodded, his gaze unwavering. "I do. There's too much smoke for there not to be a fire somewhere. I've learned to trust my gut over the years."

The words hung in the air, mingling with the scents and sounds. My journalistic instincts urged me to dig deeper and uncover the truth, while my skepticism warned me to tread gently.

The decision to explore my new town had been the right one. This experience was the life awaiting me, with endless opportunities for discovery and connection. Returning home, I arranged the fresh produce and handcrafted goodies on my kitchen counter. The colors of the fruits and vegetables radiated life, demonstrating abundance. Each item reminded me of the connections I had formed that day.

With a sense of satisfaction, I started unloading the remaining items. Handmade soaps, a jar of local honey, and a small bouquet took their place on a nearby shelf, infusing the room with a delightful aroma.

The Farmer's Market was a nice break, but the boxes were still there, reminding me of a job needing to be completed. The familiarity of my belongings contrasted with the memories of the people I encountered earlier. The laughter and warmth of conversations with Lucas and Anna played like a comforting melody. A soothing backdrop to the practicality of settling into my new space.

Elias, the enigmatic storyteller, had woven a tale of intrigue and mystery. The memory of his words lingered like a riddle that I couldn't quite shake. Skepticism warred with fascination within me, leaving me pondering the veracity of his claims.

The next day, I would visit the local library. It was the perfect place to begin my quest for answers—to dig deeper into Elias's tale, separate fact from fiction, and maybe uncover the hidden truth beneath the surface.

A week remained before my duties at the station would commence, providing me with the perfect opportunity to dive into this pursuit. Tomorrow, I would go to the local library, which had the potential to unlock secrets. It was a chance to delve deep into history and context that might uncover the mysterious story Elias wove.

Chapter 2

The gentle breeze rustled through the trees, and I stood at the library's threshold. I took a deep breath and swung open the grand double doors. The familiar aroma stirred nostalgia, returning me to the joyous moments immersed in literature.

Elias's story had aroused my curiosity. I stood on the precipice, hoping to unearth the hidden layers of dormant intrigue.

I approached the librarian's desk. A woman with silver hair and kind eyes looked up from her book and offered me a warm smile. "Good morning. How can I assist you today?"

Returning the smile, I replied, "Good morning. I'm hoping to research the history of local businesses and any possible controversies."

Her eyes sparkled with interest, and she gestured toward a nearby row of computers. "Our computer terminals have research databases that might have the information you're looking for."

"Thank you," I made my way to one of the terminals, the keyboard under my fingers a gateway to a trove of hidden stories.

The story Elias shared was like a puzzle piece waiting to fit into place. I searched the databases, scrolling through articles, archives, and historical records. The names of businesses, including cattle ranches, popped on the screen. A name kept appearing in newspaper stories and press releases in Centerville—Chris Fredrick, a cattle rancher who wielded influence far beyond his vast ranch's rolling hills.

For years, whispers of shady dealings surrounding Fredrick have been circulating, a shadow hanging over his otherwise impeccable reputation. It became clear that the circumstances behind these alleged kickbacks were rooted in a complex web of power, money, and hidden agendas.

At the center was a series of lucrative contracts for supplying beef to schools and government facilities. Fredrick's ranch held a virtual monopoly on these contracts, which were awarded without transparent bidding processes or oversight. This lack of competition allowed him to inflate prices, siphoning off significant profits while delivering subpar-quality beef to the institutions.

I delved into my research, examining business transactions and unearthing longstanding controversies. I found concrete evidence linking Fredrick to influential government and school board figures. While the evidence I uncovered was more generalized than specific, I came across financial records indicating payments made by Fredrick to these influential individuals, suggesting potential exchanges for favors or cooperation. Additionally, I found contracts and agreements outlining the terms of Fredrick's dealings with these figures, shedding light on the nature of their relationship and the benefits involved. Each discovery made it increasingly apparent that Elias's narrative might be rooted in a deeper, more intricately concealed truth. These orchestrated payoffs ensured the compliance of these individuals, intricately weaving together financial gains with the preservation of power and influence.

The librarian's words of assistance became a distant echo. It revealed an intriguing and unsettling larger picture. I was beginning to feel anxious as I followed the facts, which I knew would lead me deeper into the past of the town I was now calling home.

The clock on the wall ticked away the hours, and the afternoon sun setting towards the horizon, casting long shadows across the library's interior. My stomach rumbled, a reminder I hadn't paused for lunch.

With a sigh, I gathered my notes and pushed my chair back. I needed to take a break and reflect on the information I learned. The substandard quality of the beef supplied to schools raised concerns about food safety, and the lack of transparency in the bidding process eroded trust in officials. I was concerned about this, but I didn't know if I should be involved or pass along the information to the correct people.

I went to the librarian's desk to express my gratitude for her assistance. She looked up, her eyes twinkling with curiosity. "Did you find what you were looking for?"

I nodded, a mixture of excitement and intrigue dancing within me. "Yes, I've uncovered some interesting facts. Thank you for being so helpful."

She smiled. "Remember, the library is here to help. Don't hesitate to return if you need more information or guidance."

With a final nod of appreciation, I stepped out of the library and into the fading afternoon light. The sun hung in the sky, casting a warm golden glow over the quaint streets of Centerville. The gentle breeze tousled my hair and carried a medley of scents.

The café nestled just around the corner, its inviting atmosphere spilling onto the sidewalk in cozy outdoor seating. The scent of brewed coffee wafted from its open doors, mingling with the aromatic promise of baked goods. I approached the hum of conversation, and the clinking of cups added to the café's bustling charm.

Stepping inside, a wave of comforting warmth enveloped me, drawing me into the inviting interior. Rustic wooden tables, each with a unique story, were arranged, forming intimate corners where patrons gathered and shared moments of connection. The soft, ambient lighting cast a gentle enchantment over the space, creating an atmosphere of cozy tranquility.

Artwork adorning the walls added splashes of color and character, capturing the essence of the community's creative spirit. Amidst the soothing ambiance, the soft murmur of conversations intertwined like a soothing melody, creating a harmonious backdrop that eased the mind. I gravitated toward an unoccupied table by the window, where the sun's gentle rays spilled in, bathing the surroundings in a soft, golden embrace.

I wrestled with the implications of what I had learned at the library. On one hand, there was a moral imperative to act, to shine a light on the injustices hidden within the system and advocate for change. After all, if I didn't speak up, who would? On the other hand, getting involved meant stepping into the fray, potentially putting myself at odds with powerful interests and facing backlash from those who preferred to keep the status quo intact.

I weighed the pros and cons carefully, considering the risks and rewards of each course of action. Getting involved could mean making a difference, standing up for what was right, and fighting for the safety and well-being of our children. But it could also mean drawing unwanted attention, facing pushback from those with vested interests, and risking my reputation and livelihood.

A waitress approached my table with a warm smile, a pad, and a pen. "Welcome to Centerville Café. My name's Chelsea, and I'll care for you today. Can I start you off with something to drink?"

"Hello," I replied with a genuine smile, appreciating her friendly demeanor. "I'll have a green tea, please."

"Coming right up!" she chirped, jotting down my order. "Are you interested in trying one of our daily pastries? We have a delightful blueberry scone that's been a hit today."

The mention of the blueberry scone sparked my interest, and I nodded in agreement. "Sounds wonderful. I'll have a blueberry scone as well."

Chelsea headed toward the counter, a thought crossed my mind, a perfect opportunity to gather more information about Fredrick and the rumors swirling around him. In a few moments, she returned with my green tea and scone.

"Thank you," I said as she placed the items before me. "I caught wind of gossip at the farmer's market. Have you heard anything about a cattle rancher and kickbacks through the town gossip?"

Chelsea's eyebrows lifted, and she regarded me with a thoughtful expression. "Oh, you must be new in town. People talk about questionable dealings, but rumors can spread like wildfire."

Her words confirmed the suspicions I had been piecing together. "Has anyone looked into these rumors?"

She shrugged, a knowing smile on her lips. "Plenty of folks have talked about it, but no one's taken the plunge. Everyone's waiting for a hero to come along and unveil the truth. It's a small town, and sometimes people fear stirring the pot too much."

I thanked her for the insight, sensing the delicate balance of caution and curiosity surrounding the topic. I savored the last bite of my blueberry scone. Elias's rumors at the farmers market may be rumors, but the information about Fredrick must be looked at further. Smiling, I knew who could help me.

I reached for my phone and tapped open the messaging app. A familiar group chat awaited my attention—Samantha, Holli, and Rebeccah—the three pillars of friendship who stood by my side. Our lives took us on different paths, but our bond remained as strong as ever.

I began typing, my fingers dancing across the screen as I poured my thoughts into the text message:

"Hey, my amazing trio! It's been way too long since we hung out together. How about a little reunion soon? I have some news to share and can't wait to catch up with my favorite heroes! "

A surge of anticipation washed over me as I hit the send button. I almost heard their voices and laughter echoing in my mind, a chorus of support which seen us through countless adventures.

Almost immediately, the replies began to pour in:

Samantha: "Breanna!! You have no idea how much I've been craving a girls' night. News? Spill the beans, girl!"

Holli: "Count me in, Bre! It's been ages since our epic hangouts. Can't wait!"

Rebeccah: "Oh my gosh, yes!! I'm in dire need of some quality time with my favorite people. Share the deeds, Breanna!"

Their enthusiasm was palpable through the screen, and I couldn't help but smile. These women stood by me through every challenge, celebrated with me in times of triumph, and shared in the highs and lows of life.

I typed out my response:

"Yay, you're all in! How about we meet at my apartment this weekend in Centerville? Can't wait to catch up and share details of my new town. Love you all! "

I closed my phone with a satisfied smile and slipped it back into my pocket. The exchange with Samantha, Holli, and Rebeccah left me invigorated and eager for the weekend reunion. It was comforting that our bond remained unbreakable no matter where life took us.

Leaving the cozy ambiance of the cafe, I stepped out onto the bustling sidewalk. The sun's warm embrace greeted me, casting a golden glow over the streets of Centerville. The gentle breeze carried a sense of promise, and I took a moment to soak in the sights and sounds of the town that was becoming my home.

Reconnecting with my friends brought a fresh wave of energy. Arriving home, I paused at the threshold of my apartment. The remaining boxes reminded me of the work ahead, a tangible representation of my journey. Emotions swirled within me—a mixture of anticipation, nostalgia, and a hint of exhaustion.

I took a deep breath, allowing the familiarity of my space to wash over me. With renewed strength, I picked up where I left off, emptying items and finding their rightful places.

My mind couldn't help but drift back to the stories I encountered—the tale of Elias and the intriguing conspiracy theory he shared. The memory of his words lingered; curiosity tugged at my thoughts. I prioritized the boxes today, and the promise of further exploration remained constant. This whisper beckoned me to unravel the mysteries lying beneath the surface.

My day at the library proved Elias' story. I surveyed the room with a sense of satisfaction. The apartment began taking shape, and stories were waiting to be uncovered in its corners and crevices. The emotions accompanying me throughout the day were woven into the space's fabric.

I sank into a chair, allowing a contented sigh to escape my lips. The day was a whirlwind of connections—connecting with old friends, encountering new faces, and finally creating a sense of home in an unfamiliar place.

I checked the time and realized it was getting late. Messaging Holli, Rebeccah, and Samantha would have to wait. I needed rest, so I headed to my bedroom and turned off the light.

Chapter 3

Saturday morning arrived with a soft caress of sunlight filtering through the curtains. Stepping into the kitchen, the aroma surrounded me, mingling with the faint scent of pastries. The gentle chime of the doorbell echoed through the apartment. With a smile, I went to the door, my heart swelling with anticipation. I swung the door open, and the faces of my friends greeted me, each a source of familiarity.

"Samantha, Holli, Rebeccah!" I exclaimed, my voice brimming with delight. "It's so good to see you all again! How are my old stomping grounds of Sunnyville?"

The three women stood before me, their smiles mirroring my enthusiasm, as we stood on my doorstep - a long-overdue reunion. We all hugged together, highlighting the closeness we shared.

I ushered my friends inside, closing the door behind them. "I've missed you all."

Settling around the table, I poured cups of fragrant coffee. The spread of delectable breakfast treats beckoned an invitation to indulge in food. Laughter bubbled forth, weaving a tapestry of ease and friendship as if time had never kept us apart.

"Absolutely!" Holli exclaimed, her eyes alight with excitement. "It feels like forever since we've all been together like this."

Samantha nodded in agreement, her smile reflecting the sentiment. "I couldn't agree more," she chimed in. "There's just something special about our get-togethers. It's so good to see everyone again."

My warm voice joined the chorus. "It is. And it's like no time has passed at all. I love how we can pick up where we left off."

Holli leaned forward, curiosity shining in her eyes. "So, what's been happening lately?"

"Oh, you know," Samantha replied with a playful grin, "The usual. Work, life, trying to find time for some fun in between by programming a toaster."

Laughter erupted around the table.

Turning my attention to Holli, I couldn't help but offer a sympathetic smile. "Holli, I am so sorry about you and John."

Her response was a mix of resignation and reflection, which held a glimpse into her heart. "It just wasn't meant to be," she shared, tinged with emotions. "He's a good man, but sometimes, even goodness can't mend what's broken."

Her candidness resonated with me, a reminder of life's complexities and the unforeseen turns it often took. "I understand," I replied.

"So, Breanna," Rebeccah's voice carried a note of intrigue, her eyes gleaming with curiosity. "You mentioned having some news to share. Don't keep us in suspense!"

Leaning in, I shared, "I've only been here for a week, but already I've met some interesting people. And I caught wind of the local gossip. I couldn't resist investigating the matter, so I went to the library to uncover the truth. Even this quaint town isn't immune to corruption, and it reached even the authorities."

Samantha's brow furrowed as she questioned, "But why get involved? It doesn't relate to you or your new job."

"Would your involvement jeopardize your position before you even go on the air?" Rebeccah's concern was palpable as she voiced the potential risks.

I answered, "It could, but I also have to weigh the effects on the children and the transparency among the school board members and city leaders. This has been swept under the rug for a long time, and I am not sure people know about it. I can't say how it might affect my position. It's a matter of ethics for me. It goes against everything I stand for."

I shared the details of my investigation into shady dealings, alleged kickbacks, and the web of influence that permeated Centerville's institutions. I described the research I did at the library and how I found the contracts, the involvement of key figures, and the potential implications for the community.

Samantha's eyes widened. "Wow, Breanna, that's some heavy stuff. You're onto something here. There's more to this story than meets the eye."

Later that morning, the sun climbed higher in the sky; we decided to venture out into the heart of Centerville. We left my apartment each of us smiling and laughing as we began down the sidewalk. The soft hum of activity filled the air as locals and visitors went about their day. Samantha, Holli, Rebeccah, and I strolled along the cobblestone paths, their footsteps in harmony with their lively ambiance.

Our footsteps echoed against the pavement as we passed charming storefronts of Centerville's local businesses. The tantalizing aroma of baked goods wafted from the corner bakery, tempting our senses and eliciting an involuntary smile. Children's laughter echoed from the nearby park, indicating that families were making the most of the beautiful day.

As we continued our walk, we met some friendly faces and got some greetings at every turn. The townspeople radiated a genuine sense of community, their smiles welcoming, and their friendly conversations heartwarming.

Amid the cheerful chatter, we learned about the weekend's festivities that had the town abuzz. A kindly elderly gentleman who introduced himself as Ralph Phillips, his eyes twinkling with a lifetime of stories. We engaged in a discussion, his weathered face lit up with enthusiasm, eager to share the stories about the annual Centerville Harvest Festival. Ralph began, "Well, the Harvest Festival is a tradition around these parts. It's a time when the whole town comes alive with joy and camaraderie. The fairgrounds transform into a bustling hub of activity. Folks from far and wide gather to celebrate our community."

Ralph's words portrayed the festivities. He described the colorful parades that marched through the streets, featuring decorated floats and cheerful marching bands. His eyes twinkled as he recalled children's faces painted as they awaited the parade's arrival.

"Music fills the air, my dear friends," Ralph continued, "with live performances from local bands, your feet tapping, and singing. Let's not forget the food! The aromas of cooked delights – from corn on the cob to apple pies tickle your senses and make your mouth water."

I smiled and expressed gratitude, "Thank you so much for sharing these wonderful stories and insights with us. We appreciate your hospitality and the glimpse you've given us of the Harvest Festival. It sounds like an incredible event, and we're looking forward to experiencing it firsthand."

Ralph's eyes crinkled with a smile as he nodded, "It's been my pleasure, dear ladies. I'm glad I shared a piece of Centerville's heart. Enjoy the festival, and don't hesitate to reach out if you need anything during your stay."

Passing by the town square, we were captivated with a group of musicians playing lively tunes on a makeshift stage. The melodies in the breeze drew people in with their infectious rhythms.

Walking through the quaint streets of Centerville, I couldn't help but feel a sense of déjà vu as the familiar café came into view. Its lights spilled onto the sidewalk, and the aroma of coffee beckoned us inside. My heart raced with anticipation—we hoped Chelsea would be working today.

We entered. The soft jingle of the bell greeted us. The cozy interior embraced us like an old friend. Patrons chatted over their drinks, creating a soothing backdrop. The excitement among us was palpable as we exchanged pleasantries with Chelsea at the counter. We requested a booth. Our awaited moment arrived; she called over her co-worker to tend to her tables.

She joined us with a warm smile. Her presence was a reassuring link to our previous encounters. Conversation flowed but with a knowing glint in her eye. Chelsea leaned in, her voice a conspiratorial whisper as she revealed more about Fredrick. Chelsea's eyes sparkled as if she was about to divulge a secret. "People say he's been funding campaigns and supporting initiatives. In return, he might have some influence over certain decisions that benefit his ranch and businesses."

My mind raced as I absorbed this new piece of information. "So, there's a possibility that he's using his financial influence to gain favors and push through his agenda?"

Chelsea nodded, her expression grave. "It's all speculation. No one has been able to prove anything concrete. I said people here tend to tread carefully when confronting someone as influential as Fredrick."

We stepped outside the café, the weight of the revelations still fresh in our minds. I took a deep breath and broached the subject brewing within me. I looked at my friends and broke our silence. "So, ladies, after hearing all this, are you willing to investigate this matter with me?"

Holli's determined, unwavering voice cut through the air, "Count me in. This goes beyond a simple investigation."

Holli's resolute words hung in the air; the unspoken decision resonated with us. Samantha nodded in agreement. Rebeccah exchanged a knowing look with me, expressing her support without words.

The walk back home was exciting and full of camaraderie. The sun shone over Centerville, painting the streets with shades of gold as we strolled along the sidewalk. Laughter punctuated our conversation, reflecting our bond and the thrilling prospects ahead.

We walked and couldn't help but discuss Chelsea's wealth of information. Each step solidified our resolve, and the more we talked, the more precise our plan became. Animated discussions and playful banter echoed through the air, friendship resonating with every footfall.

***

We couldn't contain our excitement as we planned for the Harvest Festival. We were eager to immerse ourselves in the festivities. The prospect of indulging in local delicacies, exploring the vibrant stalls, and partaking in the celebrations filled us with anticipation.

Giggles filled the air as we debated which attractions to prioritize and which treats to sample first. The atmosphere had a sense of adventure, a shared excitement for the experiences that awaited us. We approached my doorstep. The joyfulness and animated discussions showed no signs of waning.

The drive to the festival grounds was full of anticipation. A burst of color and activity greeted us as we approached the entrance. The fairgrounds buzzed with energy, the air alive with the scent of delicious food, the strains of live music, and families.

We strolled through the bustling grounds, and our senses were treated to a medley of experiences. Our eyes feasted on the visual splendor. Stalls lined the pathways, offering various handcrafted goods, from intricate jewelry to woven textiles. The tantalizing aroma of cooked delicacies wafted through the air, making our mouths water.

Our ears delighted in the melodic sounds. The warmth of friendship and the spirit of togetherness permeated the air, and we couldn't help but take in the charm of it all. Children's screams and laughter echoed from the carnival rides area, where lit attractions and games beckoned with promises of fun and excitement. The stage, adorned with seasonal decorations, showcased local talents performing folk songs and dances, adding a touch of cultural richness to the festivities.

A familiar sight drew my attention as we explored the offerings and absorbed the traditions. Lucas and Anna. Their faces lit up as they spotted us, and I introduced them to my friends.

"Hey! Look who I've stumbled upon," I greeted with a grin.

Rebeccah, Holli, and Samantha exchanged warm smiles and friendly hellos as if we were reuniting with old friends.

Lucas laughed, a twinkle in his eye. "Well, this is a pleasant surprise! It's like our paths are destined to cross again."

Anna nodded in agreement, her voice filled with enthusiasm. "It's great you are all here."

We engaged in light banter, catching up on recent events and sharing anecdotes, I seized the opportunity to steer the conversation toward our ongoing investigation. "By the way, we've been investigating some interesting matters. Have you heard anything about a certain Chris Fredrick?" I asked, my tone casual but my curiosity unmistakable.

Lucas and Anna exchanged subtle glances before they responded. "Chris Fredrick, huh? Yeah, his name made its rounds," he replied, a knowing smile on his lips.

She chimed in, her expression thoughtful. "Oh. It's one of those topics that people in town can't help but discuss, even in hushed tones."

I leaned in, my interest piqued. "Are there any specific details or stories you've come across? We're trying to piece together a more comprehensive picture."

Lucas shrugged a hint of intrigue in his eyes. "It's speculation. People wonder about his connections and possible dealings, but nothing concrete has surfaced."

She nodded in agreement. "You have to be careful."

"Yes, I understand." I said, "We're simply intrigued. Anyway, enjoy the festivities."

The sun dipped below the horizon, transforming into a mesmerizing realm illuminated by twinkling lights. We bid Lucas and Anna farewell amidst the enchanting backdrop, our promises of staying connected carried away on the gentle evening breeze. The glow of lanterns and fairy lights created a magical atmosphere, casting a soft radiance over the surroundings.

We ventured toward the area where the local high school's Future Farmers of America program set up a livestock display. The soft illumination danced on the pens and enclosures, lending an almost ethereal quality to the scene. Laughter and chatter still filled the air, a symphony of nighttime revelry.

Holli's eyes gleamed with wonder as we approached a pen where baby goats frolicked, their antics illuminated. Samantha's curiosity piqued. She began a conversation with an FFA student who shared insights into the animals' care and the meaningful role of the program. The gentle hoot of an owl nearby added a touch of wild magic to the moment.

Rebeccah's fascination with horses drew us to a majestic mare, her coat shimmering under the soft lights. A young rider guided the horse through graceful movements, their connection evident in the unspoken bond between humans and animals. It was a scene of quiet beauty that resonated with us.

My attention was captivated by a group of students tending to a collection of sturdy cattle. The soft glow of the lights cast a gentle radiance on their faces as they interacted with the animals, a tableau of youthful determination and rural charm. Among them stood a tall figure at 6'1" with an air of confidence that drew my gaze. His short black hair framed his face, and his piercing blue eyes reflected the depth of the starlit sky. A sense of purpose resonated in his every move as he guided and mentored the students with effortless expertise.

Filled with curiosity, I drew closer, my steps guided by an unspoken interest.

Our eyes met in a moment of fleeting connection. The faintest hint of a smile graced his lips, acknowledging the shared appreciation for this unique display. With a nod, I initiated a conversation, the gentle hum serving as a melodic backdrop.

"Good evening," I greeted, my voice carrying a note of genuine interest. "You must be Aaron Roberts."

The man's name carried a reputation that matched his role – the town's respected veterinarian. His presence exuded a quiet authority, and his interaction with the students and the animals suggested a genuine passion for his work.

He met my gaze with a friendly nod. "That's right. You are...?"

"Breanna," I replied, extending my hand. His firm handshake conveyed a sense of friendship. We were two individuals brought together by a shared connection to the world of animals and community.

"It's a pleasure, Breanna," he said, his tone warm and welcoming. "Are you enjoying yourself?"

"Yes, I am," I responded, blushing.

A moment of contemplative silence, our gazes drifting toward the students who continued to engage with the cattle. Our conversation began to wind down, and a sense of friendship settled between us, created by insights and a mutual appreciation for the festival's charm. The soft rustle of the evening breeze played a gentle melody, intermingling with the distant hum of music filled the air.

Aaron's blue eyes held a warm spark as he offered a genuine smile. "Well, I'm glad we had the chance to chat. I hope we have the chance to run into each other again."

"I would like that," I replied, a sense of gratitude lacing my words. Our handshake held a lingering connection, a bridge between two individuals who connected over common interests.

We parted ways. My steps carried me away from the cattle display, but my thoughts remained tethered to the intriguing man I had just met. He had an aura of mystery, a quiet confidence hinting at layers beneath the surface. It wasn't just his expertise as the town's veterinarian that drew me in; it was how he spoke, listened, and showed genuine interest in our conversation.

I couldn't deny that I was smitten by him, captivated by his presence and how he carried himself. It wasn't just his physical appearance – though his tall frame and striking blue eyes were appealing – but the authenticity radiated from within. The encounter left an indelible mark, igniting a spark in my thoughts.

The festival's energy again enveloped me. Laughter echoed through the air, and the vibrant colors of the fairgrounds shimmered with an added brilliance. I shared a knowing smile with Holli, who had been watching us from a distance, her eyes filled with playful curiosity.

Chapter 4

The room was a picture of serenity, with Samantha, Holli, and Rebeccah nestled in various corners, each lost in their dreams. With a contented sigh, I stretched and rose from my makeshift bed, the carpet beneath my feet a welcome contrast to the crisp morning air.

I prepared a simple breakfast spread: pastries, fresh fruit, and steaming cups of tea. One by one, my friends began to wake up, their movements slow and deliberate as they emerged from their sleep. Groggy smiles greeted me as they joined me at the table, their eyes carrying the traces of dreams and the anticipation of a new day.

"Good morning," I greeted a gentle melody filling the room. "How did everyone sleep?"

A yawn accompanied Samantha's response, her fingers reaching for tea. "Like a log, but I needed this."

Holli nodded in agreement, her hair tousled from sleep."Agreed. Breanna, you have a gift for making mornings cozy."

Rebeccah's eyes sparkled as she joined in, her voice hard to understand because of the stretching and yawning. "Thank you for having us over, Breanna."

Friendship filled the room, a comforting backdrop to the day's intentions. Our cups of tea became vessels of connection as we settled into the morning's rhythm, recounting the previous day's events and discussing the paths ahead.

My friends and I sat around the table. I drifted into memories of our conversation at the Harvest Festival.

"Breanna," Samantha said, "Is everything okay?"

I shook my head, trying to regain my focus. "Oh, yes, sorry. I was lost in thought for a moment."

Holli shot me a knowing glance, and I could see a playful glint in her eyes. "Lost in thought about a certain someone, perhaps?"

My cheeks flushed, and I laughed. "What? No, we talked, that's all."

Rebeccah leaned in, her grin widening. "Leaving you blushing and smiling like a teenager."

I felt a mixture of embarrassment and amusement as I tried to downplay the significance of our interaction. "Come on, guys, it's not a huge deal. We're here to focus on the task at hand, remember?"

They continued to tease me. I couldn't deny the truth in their words. Yes, I was intrigued by Aaron, captivated by his presence and the easy way we talked. Amidst the excitement of unraveling the town's mysteries, I had to remind myself to keep my emotions in check.

"It's incredible how our paths have led us to this point," Samantha mused, her eyes alight with wonder. Who would have thought a simple visit to a farmer's market could unravel such a complex mystery?"

Holli's eyes sparkled, her voice laced with intrigue."Now we find ourselves on the brink of uncovering something that could have far-reaching implications for the town."

Rebeccah's eyes held interest. "So, what's the plan for today? Do we start investigating?"

Samantha's laptop glowed on the coffee table, its screen displaying various documents and research we had gathered so far. The room was bathed in the light of table lamps.

"Alright, team," I began, my voice carrying a sense of anticipation. We've heard the rumors, but now it's time to gather concrete evidence. Samantha, what have you managed to dig up?"

Samantha leaned forward, her fingers dancing across the keyboard. "I've been tracing financial connections and cross-referencing campaign contributions. Chris Fredrick's name was a donor to various political campaigns aligned with certain key figures in town."

Rebeccah nodded, furrowing her brow. "So, he's funneling money into campaigns to gain influence?"

Samantha nodded in agreement. "That's the working theory. It's a common tactic and worth investigating how these contributions might link to specific decisions or policies."

Holli chimed in, her legal expertise coming into play."We can establish a pattern of financial support followed by favorable outcomes for Fredrick. We might have a stronger case."

I leaned back in my chair, absorbing their insights. "Agreed. Let's also explore any direct connections between him and the local authorities. Are there any instances of them collaborating on projects or initiatives?"

Rebeccah tapped her fingers on the table, lost in thought."I'll dig into any public records or documents that might illuminate these collaborations. They may have been careful to keep their dealings off the radar, but we might find something."

The hum of laptops created a soothing backdrop as we navigated through the digital world, unearthing data fragments that promised to unveil hidden truths. Fingers glided across keyboards, producing a symphony of tapping sounds, while sporadic murmurs of conversation and quiet contemplation punctuated the air. We delved deeper. I stumbled upon a name that caught my attention—Joyce Black.

"Hey, guys," I called out, my voice tinged with excitement and intrigue.

Rebeccah, Holli, and Samantha gathered around as I pointed to the name. "Joyce Black was a prominent figure in Centerville about a decade ago," I explained. "She was famous for her philanthropic endeavors and community involvement."

Holli furrowed her brow. "So, what's the twist?"

I took a deep breath. "Well, Joyce was a vocal advocate for transparency and accountability in local government. She spearheaded efforts to uncover potential corruption."

Samantha's eyes widened. "Are you saying she might have been investigating the same issues we are now?"

I nodded. "Here's where it gets even more intriguing. In these records, Joyce's investigations might have led her to something that could have exposed individuals and their illicit activities."

"What happened to her? Did she uncover anything?" Rebeccah asked.

I flipped through more records until I found a newspaper clipping from years ago. The headline read, "Prominent Activist Joyce Black Missing Under Mysterious Circumstances."

"According to this article," I explained, "She disappeared without a trace, leaving behind a community shocked and bewildered by her sudden absence. Her whereabouts remained unknown despite extensive searches and investigations, and the case went cold."

Holli's eyes narrowed. "So, you're suggesting Joyce's investigation might have led her too close to the truth, and someone might have silenced her?"

"It's a possibility we can't ignore," I replied, my voice tinged with concern. "Joyce was indeed onto something. Her disappearance might be linked to the corruption we're trying to uncover."

We realized our research had taken an even more ominous turn. Joyce Black's story added a layer of urgency. We were not uncovering a web of corruption. We were tracing the footsteps of someone who walked this path before us.

Holli stretched her arms above her head, a satisfied smile on her face. "I think we're onto something here. The more we discovered, the more like a real pattern of manipulation and backroom dealings."

Samantha concurred, " Though we're not alone in this, we must be careful. To confront those involved, we need solid, undeniable evidence."

My mind already racing with ideas for the next steps. "Agreed. Let's continue digging, gathering as much evidence as we can. We'll need to be strategic about how we approach this."

Amidst our collective effort to process the newfound information, a gentle voice broke through the concentration. Holli's eyes met mine as she leaned forward, a hint of concern in her gaze.

"Breanna, you with us?" Her words were a lifeline, grounding me in the present during a crucial moment of discussion.

I blinked, refocusing my attention on her. "Yes, sorry. Got lost in thought again."

Holli grinned. "Thinking about Aaron, I assume?"

I chuckled, a mixture of embarrassment and amusement."Yeah, I guess he's been on my mind."

As the day passed, I struggled to balance my determination to uncover the truth and the magnetic pull of a potential romance. It was like walking a tightrope, trying to stay focused on the research while allowing myself to explore this newfound connection.

Holli leaned in, her voice soft. "Remember, Breanna, it's okay to have feelings, even amidst all this chaos."

The air buzzed with the gentle symphony of rustling papers, murmured discussions, and laptop clicks. Around the table, maps and documents were sprawled, waiting for discovery.

I nodded, grateful for her understanding. "I know its a lot to process."

We wrapped up our weekend of research in a room that was a blend of accomplishment and expectation. The fading afternoon sunlight painted warm hues on the walls, creating a cozy haven for our deliberations.

The time approached to part ways, a bittersweet sentiment lingered. Holli, Rebeccah, and Samantha would each carry a portion of our investigation, nurturing it like a seed that would bloom further next weekend. The prospect of our next gathering held a promise of progress. Holli's ability to dissect every line of public reports resonated with me. Her pursuit of discrepancies and hidden clues were akin to a detective unraveling a complex case.

Rebeccah's plan to delve deeper into Joyce's story intrigued me. Joyce's story contained a wealth of untapped knowledge, and I saw Rebeccah's knack for extracting information as invaluable. With her digital prowess, Samantha stood ready to discover electronic breadcrumbs that could bring us closer to the truth. My debut as a broadcaster approached, my friends' encouraging words uplifted my spirits.

Their promise to tune in and support me on my big day was a major source of inspiration.

A brief hush settled over my apartment as the door clicked shut, allowing me to embrace the ambiance surrounding me. The traces of our intensive investigation adorned every corner. An array of documents and clues mirrored our unwavering commitment. A mosaic of determination etched into the very essence of the room.

The prospect of stepping into the broadcasting world the next day added an extra layer of complexity, entangling my thoughts in a whirlwind of possibilities.

I stood there, absorbing the energy lingering from our collective endeavor; a sense of purpose crystallized. Tomorrow would be challenging in many ways, and I was ready to seize every opportunity, no matter how daunting.

Chapter 5

The thrill of my endeavors merged seamlessly with the prospect of addressing the town through the screen. I selected my outfit for my debut, aiming to strike a delicate balance between professionalism and approachability. Stepping into a role necessitates authority and a genuine connection to the community.

Leaving my apartment behind, I drove through the familiar streets of Centerville. The world around me pulsed with energy, as if the town sensed the day's significance. The drive to the station was a mixture of anticipation and reflection. The familiar exterior of the KBNR building and its modern architecture stood as a beacon of information and connection.

The sight of the KBNR sign filled me with awe. The early morning sunlight cast a glow on the building's glass façade. With a steadying breath, I gathered my belongings and went to the entrance. The lobby exuded polished professionalism combined with bustling energy. The soft murmur of voices and footsteps echoed through the space, creating a sense of purposeful activity. The reception desk had a sleek arrangement of flowers, a touch of warmth contrasted with the pristine white walls and modern décor.

My heart pounded excitedly, and I kept biting my upper lip, something I had always done to ease my nerves. The receptionist greeted me. Her friendly demeanor put me at ease. "Good morning! I am Claudia, and you must be Breanna, our new morning anchor. Welcome to KBNR."

Her words were a balm to my nerves, and I nodded."Thank you so much. I'm excited to be here."

Claudia handed me a temporary badge and directions to the make-up room and studio. Upon entering the room, I heard friendly greetings from the artists already working. The room was abuzz with activity, with mirrors and cosmetics spread across tables, and the soft glow of vanity lights illuminated each station.

"Morning, Breanna!" one of the artists called out, her smile inviting. We've been expecting you. Take a seat, and soon you'll be camera-ready."

I settled into the chair and marveled at the transformation underway. They worked their magic, skillfully enhancing my features while maintaining a natural and polished appearance. With the gentle brush against my skin, I relaxed in the process.

We exchanged lighthearted banter and shared stories. Laughter and easy conversation made me part of the team. We covered everything from current events to personal anecdotes, and a connection and comfort began to replace the nerves within me.

My makeup was complete, and I glanced at my reflection in the mirror. The transformation was subtle yet impactful. My features were enhanced, and my skin radiated a healthy glow. They gathered around, their approving smiles filling me with confidence.

"You look fantastic," one said with a grin. "You're going to light up the screen."

The broadcast was about to begin, and my heart quickened with excitement.

My co-anchor, John Gloush, exuded a seasoned journalist's confidence, and his presence commanded attention whenever he entered the room. Tall and composed, he was like the embodiment of an anchor. His suit was impeccable, his shirt pressed, and his hair styled—a true professional. What struck me most was his smile and approachability.

Meeting him for the first time made me feel admiration and nerves. His handshake was firm, his smile genuine, easing my apprehensions. Despite his impressive credentials and unpretentious senior status at KBNR, his attitude was reassured. Passionate about journalism, he delivered news that mattered to viewers.

Emotions surged as I settled into the chair beside him. The studio filled me with bright lights, sleek technology, and polished professionalism. The teleprompter in front of me displayed the opening lines of the morning news segment, intensifying my nerves.

The countdown began, and I took a steadying breath, my heart racing. My fingers found their place on the desk, and I glanced at him, who offered a reassuring nod. The gesture conveyed a sense of unity, bolstering my confidence. The weight of the responsibility ahead settled in, and determination surged within me, refusing to let it overwhelm me.

The red recording light blinked to life, and I drew on my training, channeling years of preparation into my delivery. Speaking with the audience through the camera's lens, my voice was steady, and my presence was poised. The initial jitters faded, replaced by a deep sense of how I drew upon my journey and utilized it.

John and I conversed seamlessly throughout the broadcast, transitioning from story to story. Evident was his expertise, from which I gleaned through his subtle cues and masterful interactions. Working alongside someone with a wealth of experience who cared about my growth as a journalist filled me with gratitude.

The show's final segment concluded, and John and I exchanged a brief but gratified smile. A sense of accomplishment lingered in the air, a shared understanding as we navigated the intricate dance of live television. The camera's red light blinked off, signaling the end of our on-screen presence, but the energy in the studio remained.

He turned to me, his expression one of genuine approval."Your presence on screen is impressive, and you handled the stories well."

A surge of gratitude washed over me. "Thank you. Your support makes a world of difference."

He chuckled. "Well, welcome to the world of morning news, Breanna. It's fast-paced and demanding, but it's also gratifying."

A friendly voice interrupted our conversation. "You two were fantastic this morning!"

I turned to Jackie, one of the makeup artists, approaching with a smile. Her presence a welcome sight, and her cheerful demeanor added a touch of warmth to the studio atmosphere.

"Thank you, Jackie," I replied, appreciative."You worked wonders. You made the process easy."

She laughed, a twinkle in her eyes. "Oh, don't worry. You are a natural in front of the camera. Don't hesitate if you need anything."

I realized the support extended beyond John and the production team. The entire environment at KBNR exuded a spirit of collaboration and encouragement, nurturing growth and allowing everyone to shine.

The studio quieted, and John and I took a moment to reflect on the morning. "Breanna," he said, his voice thoughtful, "you have a real gift for connecting with the audience. The way you delivered. It was relatable and engaging."

I surged with pride, humbled by his words, "Thank you, John. It means a lot, coming from someone with your experience."

He smiled. "Well, we make a good team with many more broadcasts together."

One of the producers asked me to discuss potential stories for the next broadcast. Excited to contribute, I was eager to share my ideas and insights. My enthusiasm for the work ahead grew as discussions swirled around breaking news, story angles, and upcoming interviews. Meanwhile, I noticed John engaged in an animated discussion with Connie, a senior producer, indicating they were deep in planning and brainstorming. Curious, I approached them, greeted warmly by John, who invited me to join their conversation.

Connie smiled, extending a hand. "It's good to have you on board, Breanna. Your debut was impressive – you have a natural presence onscreen."

I shook Connie's hand, "Thank you so much. I'm excited to join the team and contribute to the show."

It dawned on me that this endeavor transcended mere segment planning. It evolved into a collaborative process where ideas were shared, refined, and crafted into compelling stories for the audience. John's insights as a seasoned anchor were invaluable, and Connie's strategic vision added a layer of depth to the editorial process.

"We're hosting the upcoming town hall meeting," Connie explained, her eyes gleaming. It's a chance to address some of the issues we've been investigating. This will allow you to build a strong connection to the community. Your background in investigation reporting brings a unique dimension to the event."

Enthusiastic about the prospect of a significant local event. "I'd be honored to contribute."

After our planning session, I approached her.

"Connie," I began, "Can you give me more insight into what we'll cover in the future?"

She turned toward me, her expression a mix of seriousness and determination. "Of course, Breanna. We have been covering various topics, causing quite a stir in Centerville. From local events and initiatives to human interest, we aim to bring a well-rounded perspective of life in the town."

"It sounds like we're planning to capture the essence of Centerville and its people," I commented.

"Exactly," she affirmed. We believe our reporting should reflect the diverse experiences of this community's fabric. By highlighting the positive aspects, challenges, and triumphs, we can provide a comprehensive view that resonates with our viewers."

Her words resonated with the sense of purpose that had drawn me to journalism in the first place. Beyond reporting facts, there lies a deeper purpose: portraying the richness of life and forging profound connections with the audience.

"I'm thrilled to be a part of this effort," I said, my enthusiasm evident. "This is my perspective on the upcoming town hall coverage."

Connie smiled, her eyes reflecting the same determination. "We're excited to have you on board, Breanna. Your connection to the community will bring a personal touch to our reporting."

At the reception area, the receptionist, Claudia, greeted me with a friendly smile and a wave. "Great job, Breanna. You're settling into your role."

"Thank you, Claudia," I replied, returning her smile. "I appreciate your kind words."

My interactions, the nods of recognition and the smiles from strangers—were small yet meaningful reminders of our impact as broadcasters. It is a privilege to be a vehicle for information, to bridge the gap between the stories and those relying on them.

I was still a little excited about my first day at the station. I decided to go to the café, run into Chelsea, and have a fun conversation. After a few minutes, I arrived at the café. A smile came to my face as I approached the door.

The quaint café exuded an inviting charm, its cozy atmosphere a haven for those seeking respite from the bustle of the outside world. I stepped inside. Before I knew it, the familiar chime of the bell above the café's door signaled my entry into this haven of relaxation.

Approaching the counter, I met Chelsea.

"Hey, Breanna!" she greeted me, her voice infused with genuine warmth. "Is this the usual today?"

"A cup of tea and a blueberry muffin, please," I replied with a smile, appreciating her attentiveness.

She quickly prepared my order with a nod, her movements efficient yet graceful. I waited. I glanced around the café, taking in the sights and sounds of the familiar surroundings. The soft chatter of patrons, the gentle clinking of cups, and the occasional burst of laughter created a comforting symphony.

Chelsea returned with a tray with the items I ordered. "Here you go. Enjoy!" Chelsea's smile widened as she looked at me. "I caught your newscast this morning. You were fantastic!"

"Thank you so much," I replied. "I'm thrilled you enjoyed it."

Her smile widened. "It's my pleasure. Enjoy your time and, let me know if you need anything else."

With a nod of appreciation, I found a cozy corner by the window that offered a perfect vantage point for people-watching. Sipping my tea and savoring the muffin, my gaze wandered, observing the ebb and flow of activity in the café.

My heart skipped a beat. Aaron Roberts was sitting nearby. He exuded quiet confidence, commanding attention even in a busy space. My pulse quickened, and a mixture of surprise and curiosity surged. I stood and approached as if drawn by an invisible force. He looked up from his cup of coffee, his gaze meeting mine. Time stood still as our eyes locked, and a silent connection formed. The world faded away, leaving only us in this intimate moment.

Summoning my courage, I offered a tentative smile."Mind if I join you?"

Aaron's lips curved into a smile. "Please, have a seat."

Sliding into the booth across from him. The cushioned seat was comfortable, and I settled in, sipping my tea to steady my nerves.

"Breanna, right?" Aaron asked, his voice a smooth, velvety timbre resonated with warmth.

I nodded. "Yes, it's nice to see you again."

His gaze held interest. "What brings you here?"

"Actually," I began, a hint of a smile playing at the corners of my lips, "I've been meaning to ask you a few questions."

"Questions?" His eyebrows lifted in genuine interest. "I'm listening."

Leaning in, "Aaron, I hope you don't mind me bringing this up, but rumors around town about certain issues my friends and I have been investigating. Rumors of corruption and hidden dealings might connect to influential individuals here. Do you have any insights into what's been going on?"

His eyes met. He took a moment to gather his thoughts before responding, "Breanna, I can understand your curiosity. The community has been concerned about some questionable local government decisions and financial contracts."

"Can you share anything specific? Do you have any patterns or leads that might help us?" I asked, eager to uncover the truth that was evident in my voice.

Aaron's gaze held a mix of understanding and caution."I can tell you about discussions with certain individuals interested in maintaining the status quo. If I tell you, it could mean compromising the community's well-being. However, I feel I can trust you with this information."

His words seamlessly fit into the larger picture of corruption we had compiled. I nodded, absorbing the information and considering its implications.

"Have any names come up in these discussions? Individuals who might have a connection to these questionable dealings?" I hoped his insights would illuminate the key players we should focus on.

Aaron's expression turned thoughtful. "I can't give you specific names. Some of these discussions have revolved around influential figures in town—people holding positions of power and influence."

His words resonated, echoing the sentiments of Holli, Rebeccah, and Samantha. The urgency became more apparent.

I left the café in a state of quiet contemplation. The town bustled with its usual activities—people going about their day, the distant hum of traffic, and the soft rustling of leaves in the gentle breeze. Despite the familiar sights and sounds, my thoughts consumed the unexpected encounter I had just experienced.

Aaron's words lingered in my mind, adding significance to our investigation. The confirmation that there were concerning individuals within the community validated our research, reminding me that our efforts were not in vain. Aaron's revelation of possible influential people added a sense of urgency. The people who held positions within Centerville may be the key players in the wrongdoing.

Walking through the streets on my way back to KBNR, my mind raced with possibilities. How could we uncover the identities of these influential figures? We needed more than whispers and rumors—concrete evidence that could withstand scrutiny.

The town hall meeting was the perfect avenue for an open exchange of ideas. Concerned citizens could voice their opinions and share their insights, and those who perhaps had been privy to the veiled corruption could find a safe harbor to step forward.

I opened the message in our group chat with the girls.

Breanna: Did you catch my news broadcast at 5 a.m.? Curious about what you think!

The chat lit up with responses, and my heart fluttered with excitement and anticipation.

Holli: Of course! I set my alarm. You were amazing!

Samantha: You rocked it! It was fantastic!

Rebeccah: I was up early, too, and I loved every second of it! You're a natural on screen!

Their enthusiastic messages filled me with a rush of happiness. Knowing that my friends were with me, cheering me on during this new career phase, was heartwarming.

Breanna: Okay, ladies, you won't believe what happened. I bumped into Aaron Roberts, the vet. We had an interesting conversation.

Holli: Whoa, that's intriguing!

Samantha: It sounds like he may be a valuable ally. What did he say?

Rebeccah: I'm curious about any possible names.

Their thoughts echoed the thoughts swirling in my mind. The momentum was building, and seeing how everything unfolded was exciting.

Breanna: Regarding progress, KBNR is hosting a town hall meeting. A perfect opportunity. What do you think?

Holli: That's a genius plan!

Samantha: Count me in!

Rebeccah: I'm on board too.

Chapter 6

The car pulled up, and the doors closed. I rush to the window. My friends were at the front door. The air buzzed with anticipation as the four of us settled into a comfortable seating arrangement. On the counter was a folder that I picked up and began to spread all the documents out.

"What is our plan of attack for this weekend?" I asked.

"We need to start by mapping out the connections," Holli said in a steady, analytical tone. Nodding in agreement, she said her words with the precision of a seasoned investigator.

"You can include Chris Fredrick. He is at the center of everything. His influence was beyond the rolling hills of his ranch – a man townspeople say should not be reckoned with." I commented. "Trish Turner, a school board member who campaigned against using Fredrick Ranch's ground beef, sparked controversy. She won the election but lost influence on the school board."

Holli asked, "Could she have the information we need for our research?"

"Did John Gloush have anything on this?" Rebeccah inquired.

"John has connections all over this town. He would know all the details if something is going on." I commented.

Holli, meticulous in her research, had a notebook filled with her latest discoveries.

Holli began, "I've been cross-referencing their activities and financial transactions, and some patterns caught my attention. According to meeting records, Fredrick has met with school board members right before elections or votes on important proposals."

Samantha tapped her fingers on the couch's armrest, showing her growing impatience with the unfolding revelations. Rebeccah remained unwavering, her mind racing to connect the dots.

Holli's voice shattered the brief silence. "There are unexplained gaps in the financial records of Fredrick and the school board members," she revealed, her tone tinged with concern. "These gaps suggest irregularities or hidden transactions that haven't been disclosed publicly. I'm worried about what this might mean—it hints at potential financial impropriety or efforts to conceal certain activities." With a sigh, Holli concluded, "This situation is getting more complicated than I thought. It seems they were actively trying to cover their tracks."

Samantha nodded, her brow furrowed. "There is more to their finances than meets the eye."

Holli's presentation moved on to the lifestyle discrepancies and charitable donations. These leaders had betrayed that trust for personal gain. I exchanged a glance with Samantha, and her eyes mirrored my indignation.

Samantha leaned forward, her eyes sparkling with excitement. "Okay, ladies," Samantha started, her fingers dancing across the keyboard as she navigated through her findings. "This week has been quite the journey. I've been diving into the online presence of our key players."

My brows furrowed as I absorbed Samantha's words. "What did you find?"

Samantha's eyes flickered with a mix of determination and doubt. "Well, remember that local charity event last year? The one where Fredrick and Trish Turner were both in attendance? A series of photos shows them engaged in a pretty cozy embrace. That's not all. I found a trail of social media interactions between them—likes, comments, and even direct messages."

Holli's mind immediately kicked into gear. "Could those interactions be harmless? We need something concrete."

Samantha nodded, her fingers pulling up a screen filled with financial transactions. "Fredrick's donations to local charities align with decisions made by the school board members. It's as if the more money he donated, the more favorable the contracts became."

Rebeccah shifted her weight in her seat and began to lean forward. "This is strong evidence of a quid pro quo arrangement. How do we tie it all together?"

Samantha smiled. "I'm glad you asked. The encrypted email exchange? It took me a while, but I managed to decrypt it."

My eyes sparkled with excitement and resolve. "So, we have the online connections, the financial transactions, and the hidden communications. It's all pointing to a coordinated effort to maintain control and manipulate decisions."

Samantha leaned back in her chair. Satisfaction was evident in her eyes as she glanced at the screen displaying the intricate connections we had unraveled. The other women exchanged nods of approval, their focus shifting to the magnitude of their progress. Despite the task, my mind had a sense of its own, wandering back to Aaron. The conversation etched itself into my thoughts throughout the week. His words replayed like a melodic refrain.

I wondered if Aaron would have found a place in our circle, his analytical mind, and demeanor fitting seamlessly into our dynamic. His insights had a way of unraveling complexities. Lost in thought, I found myself retracing the path of our last encounter. I could not deny that my feelings for Aaron were growing. I was shocked and anxious that these feelings could move so fast and deep.

"Breanna, you have that look," Holli remarked, her tone teasing yet affectionate.

I blinked, caught off guard. "What look?"

She chuckled, leaning back against the plush cushions of the couch. "The 'you're thinking about something other than the investigation' look."

Refocusing on the discussion at hand. The intensity of my friends' gazes told me I missed a crucial point. Gathering my thoughts, I offered a brief recap of my ideas before adding, "And... I believe Aaron might have more information than he's revealing."

Rebeccah raised an eyebrow. "You think he's keeping something from us?"

Hesitating, unsure of how to articulate the complexity of my suspicions. "There was a moment during our conversation when I sensed a hesitation. It's as if he had a glimpse into the heart of this, but he chose not to divulge everything."

Samantha, her expression pensive. "So, what's our next move? Do we confront him?"

Holli chimed in, her voice a steady anchor amid the uncertainty. "Let's not determine any conclusions. We need to gather more evidence before we make any decisions. Breanna, keep an open mind."

Samantha's eyes locked onto me, her eyes alight with curiosity and relentless resolve. "What's our next move?"

Leaning in, a surge of ideas flooded my mind. "Well," I replied with unwavering composure, "I think our first order of business should be reaching out to the key players we've identified."

Rebeccah's agreement was swift and decisive. "You and I can take the lead on scheduling interviews with Trish Turner and, of course, Fredrick."

Holli's resolve added a firm note to her voice. "I'll continue cross-referencing their financial activities, hunting for irregularities or consistent patterns."

Samantha's nimble fingers crossed her keyboard, capturing our strategy in her notes. "Count me in with Holli. I'll inspect online, following any digital breadcrumbs leading us to more evidence."

Emotions stirred within me as I recognized the task's urgency. The need to talk with Aaron weighed on my mind, tugging at my thoughts like a persistent whisper. I retrieved my phone from my pocket and tapped my fingers on the screen. I typed a text message that conveyed my intentions.

Breanna: Hey Aaron. Would you be available later tonight? I have something important I'd like to discuss with you.

A flutter of uncertainty was in my chest as I pressed the send button. The seconds stretched, each clock ticking longer than the last. Like a swift response to my internal yearning, my phone illuminated with Aaron's reply. His message appeared a lifeline of connection in a sea of digital communication.

Aaron: I'm intrigued by your message. Sure, I can meet up tonight. How about that little café on Elm Street around 7 p.m.? I'm looking forward to our conversation.

A hint of a smile touched my lips.

Breanna: Sounds perfect,

Resolute fueled my steps as I shared the exchange with Rebeccah, my voice laced with resoluteness. "Aaron and I are meeting tonight."

Rebeccah's eyes gleamed with praise. "You're onto something big. Let's keep pushing forward. Speaking of which, we should also reach out to Trish Turner."

Nodding, I reached for my phone and dialed Trish's number. The anticipation hummed as the call connected, and Trish's voice filled the line. "Hello?"

"Hi, Trish. This is Breanna Willis. I want to talk about the school board's position on the safety of school lunches," I greeted her, my tone measured yet friendly. "I wanted to discuss something important about the school lunches. Can we get together with my friend Rebeccah and talk?"

There was a pause on the other end before Trish responded, her voice tinged with cautious curiosity. "I suppose I have some time. There's a coffee shop in town that I like. How about we meet there?"

My heart quickened with a renewed sense of purpose. "That sounds great, Trish. Can you give me the address?"

Hanging up the call, I turned to Rebeccah with a concluded glint in my eyes. "Trish is willing."

I stepped out of my apartment. The late afternoon sunbathed the streets of Centerville in a golden hue, and the sounds of the town welcomed us. My heart raced, tension swirling within me.

The quaint coffee shop loomed ahead, its rustic brick exterior and weathered wood exuding a charming allure. The cozy interior through the large windows – a haven of mismatched furniture, potted plants, and warm lighting. The space blended comfort and familiarity with inviting nooks adorned with books and artwork. The soothing strains of jazz music filled the air, a gentle backdrop to the hushed conversations.

The dim lighting created an intimate surrounding, allowing my focus to sharpen on the pending meeting. The gentle jingle of the coffee shop's door caught my attention, and my gaze shifted to the entrance. Trish Turner entered with a purposeful stride, her aura radiating conviction. Her dark hair framed her face, and her attire balanced professionalism and approachability.

My emotions swirled – a blend of anticipation, curiosity, and a hint of nervousness. Rebeccah's presence beside me offered reassurance, a silent reminder that we were embarking on a crucial conversation together. Trish's eyes met mine, and I greeted her as she sat across from us. The subdued lighting of the coffee shop enveloped us, lending an air of privacy to our gathering.

Rebeccah broke the silence, her tone respectful yet direct. "Thank you for meeting with us, Trish."

Trish's response measured, her attention alternating between us. "Of course. Your message intrigued me, and I'm curious about the purpose of our talk."

"We're trying to piece together the events surrounding the contracts for supplying beef to the local schools. Any insights you have are appreciated!"

Trish's features contorted with a hint of concern, her brow furrowing. Sunlight streamed through the coffee shop's windows, casting rays across the table and creating fleeting patterns of light and shadow. A quiet sigh escaped Trish's lips, and her look retreated to some distant place as though searching for the right words. "I appreciate your dedication to uncovering the truth, but I don't have any information."

Beside me, Rebeccah's voice carried a mixture of empathy and unyielding resolve. "Trish, this might be uncomfortable, but we're here to illuminate potential irregularities. Our research indicates that the circumstances around these contracts might have influenced your election to the school board. Can you elaborate on that?"

Trish's eyes widened in surprise, confusion, and disbelief. "I'm not sure what you're talking about. My campaign focused on educational reform and community engagement. I do not know any contracts."

Trish's shoulders relaxed as she gathered her belongings and walked away. The faint jingle of the doorbell punctuated the conclusion of our conversation. Exchanging a glance with Rebeccah, we shared a silent understanding that our pursuit was far from over.

Trish's figure disappeared down the sidewalk, Rebeccah said in a hushed voice. "Breanna, something isn't right. Trish was very elusive."

"I agree. Hey Rebeccah, why don't we call John Gould? He knows so much about this community and its people. Maybe he can help us."

"That sounds like a great idea."

"Ok. Let me call him," I said, reaching for my phone.

I dialed his number. After a few moments, he picked up, his voice familiar. "Hey, Breanna! How's it going?"

"Hi, John," I replied, trying to sound composed despite my excitement. "I was wondering if we could meet up. It's about something related to the town, and I think your insight would be helpful."

There was a brief pause on the other end, and I could almost picture John's thoughtful expression. "Breanna. I'm always happy to help. What's the best time for you?"

"How about this afternoon? How about the coffee shop on Elm Street? Would that work for you?" I asked.

John's response was almost immediate, his eagerness palpable through the phone. "That sounds perfect. I've got some time today".

Checking the time and calculating how long it would take us to arrive. "Could you make it in about 20 minutes?"

"See you then," He confirmed.

Rebeccah and I made our way. The minutes stretched as we found a table near the window and kept an eye on the entrance. Time ticked by, and just as I wondered if he would make it, the café's door swung open. John Gloush, his tall figure striding into the shop, scanned the room before his eyes settled on us, and a smile spread across his face.

"Hey ladies," John greeted, taking a seat. "What's this all about?."

Rebeccah started, "We just want to know if you know anything about the Fredrick contracts and rumored kickbacks."

John's expression shifted from curiosity to worry. "Whoa, slow down," he interjected. "You two are digging into some dangerous territory. The rumors you're talking about are not something you should be poking around in."

Rebeccah's analytical gaze fixed on him. "What do you mean?"

John's eyes held a hint of gravity as he cautioned, "Sometimes, the truth can come with consequences. They won't hesitate to protect their interests."

A chill ran down my spine as John's words sank in. "Are you saying you know about this?" I asked, my voice tinged with urgency.

John's lips formed a tight line, his expression a mixture of concern and warning. "I'm not saying I know anything specific. I've overheard enough whispers to understand this path is dangerous. You two should be careful."

John's gaze met ours, "Consider this a friendly warning. Just be cautious. The deeper you dig, the more you might unearth things that are better left buried."

His words lingered, and a heavy silence settled between Rebeccah and me. Two encounters, two dead ends, and now, a cryptic warning that hinted at potential danger.

Rebeccah's mind dissected every word he had spoken. Her eyes, sharp and focused, now held a hint of concern. Realizing our pursuit may have real consequences was sobering. The evasive Trish Turner and the cautious John Gloush—loomed in my mind. What were they hiding? Why were they so adamant about steering us away?

Our next step had to be a confrontation with Fredrick himself. We needed answers. Anyone held the key to unraveling this web of corruption, it was him. The plan formed, anticipation, anxiety, and adrenaline coursed through us. The prospect of facing the influential cattle rancher was both exciting and nerve-wracking.

My fingers gripped my phone as I dialed Fredrick's number. The ringing on the other end stretched into eternity before a voice answered. It was him—the man at the center of it all.

"Mr. Fredrick," I began, my voice steady despite the butterflies fluttering in my stomach. "My name is Breanna Willis, and I'm an investigative journalist. I've been looking into certain matters involving your ranch, and I was hoping we could meet to discuss them."

His response was deliberate, his tone guarded. "Why would I meet up with a journalist?"

I continued. "It's in your best interest to hear what we have to say."

He relented and provided an address. The conversation ended, and we drove for 40 minutes to the ranch.

Stepping out of the car and facing grandeur, a rush of emotions surged through me. The sprawling expanse was a beautiful display of rustic elegance and luxury. The house, a grand structure of rich wood and stone, exuded an air of authority and means that was impossible to ignore. The manicured gardens and pristine pathways beckoned us forward.

With a deep breath, Rebeccah raised her hand and knocked. The door swung open, revealing a middle-aged woman.

"Good afternoon, may I help you?" the woman inquired. I glanced at Rebeccah before stepping forward.

"We're here to meet with Mr. Fredrick," I explained, my voice steady.

The woman regarded us for a moment before nodding and stepping aside. "Please, come in. Mr. Fredrick is aware of your arrival."

The mansion's interior was just as lavish as its exterior. Rich furnishings and tasteful decor adorned the space, creating an ambiance of refined luxury. We followed the woman through the hallway, I couldn't shake that we were venturing into the lion's den. Stepping into a world where power and influence reign supreme.

Soon, we found ourselves in an appointed sitting room, the atmosphere blending elegance and tension. Rebeccah and I exchanged a firm glance. We settled into our seats, the door opened again, and Fredrick entered the room.

He was a formidable figure, exuding a commanding presence that demanded attention. His piercing gaze swept over us, reminding us we were treading on delicate ground.

"Mr. Fredrick, thank you for seeing us."

Fredrick's response was a masterful display of poise and confidence, tailored to present himself as a responsible and reputable figure within Centerville. He leaned forward, his hands resting on the polished surface of the desk, exuding an air of sincerity.

"Ladies, I appreciate your concern for the well-being of our community," Chris began, his voice confident. "My success in this town resulted from hard work, dedication, and fair competition. I've always operated within the bounds of the law and upheld the highest ethical standards."

His eyes held mine for a moment, a challenge hidden behind his polite exterior. It was as if he dared me to question the integrity of a man who amassed wealth and influence. I was not swayed, and a rehearsed speech couldn't dismiss the evidence we gathered.

"We're not here to cast judgment, Mr. Fredrick," Rebeccah interjected, her voice calm but resolute.

Fredrick's smile widened, a gesture of conciliation that masked his underlying resolve. "Of course, I am more than willing to cooperate with any investigation. I have nothing to hide, and I believe the truth will speak for itself."

The alleged kickbacks and questionable contracts were not mentioned head-on. His commitment to transparency was a strategic move to deflect from the significant part.

Rebeccah's astute questioning continued, probing for cracks in Fredrick's narrative. Her inquiries delved into the specific financial transactions that raised suspicions, the connections between key players, and the alleged discrepancies had become known. With each question, Chris's confidence wavered, revealing glimpses of a man who may not be as untouchable as he portrayed himself.

Leaving his home, his crafted words lingered in the air, a challenge for us to untangle the web of secrecy that surrounded him. Fredrick's response served as a starting point, a glimpse into the complex layers of corruption that we believed lay beneath the surface of Centerville. Our path forward was clear—to peel back those layers, challenge his narrative, and uncover the truth that remained hidden for far too long.

Chapter 7

Rebeccah and I returned to my apartment. My door creaked open, and we stepped inside, greeted by the familiar coziness of our shared space. Holli and Samantha sat on the couch, their presence a comforting sight.

"Hey, you two," Samantha said in her soothing voice, a balm to the turmoil in our minds. "How did it go? We've been waiting to hear all about your interviews."

A grateful smile tugged at the corners of my lips. Rebeccah settled in next to me, and we shared a collective sigh.

"It was intense," I began. "Our conversations with Trish, John, and Chris were like puzzle pieces that won't fit together."

Holli asked, "What did they say? Did you find any leads?"

Rebeccah sighed. "Trish was holding back something. There's a gap between what she knows and what she's willing to reveal."

"John is cautious. He hinted at hidden dangers and Chris's dealings but stopped short of concrete details."

Samantha's brows furrowed, and her systematic mind dissected what we described. "Fredrick? What did he have to say?"

I responded, "Chris played his cards close to his chest. He moved around our questions, projected an image of innocence."

Holli's voice held a spark of encouragement. "Dead ends can be discouraging, but they're also signposts of a deeper mystery."

"What did you find while we were out?" I asked, my voice eager.

"We started by looking into Fredrick's financial records. We found nothing incriminating but a pattern of large payments to a consulting firm with ties to some local officials." Holli said.

Samantha chimed in, her words weaving a tapestry of intrigue. "It's not a direct link, but the date and amounts of these payments raise some questions. Given the scheduling of important decisions and contracts."

I looked at Rebeccah, "Are these payments related to the alleged kickbacks or a way to funnel money?"

Holli nodded. "It's a possibility. We're working on tracing the flow of funds further, but it's a complex, tangled web."

Rebeccah's gaze locked onto mine. "What about Trish Turner?"

Samantha's smile held a hint of satisfaction. "We uncovered connections between Trish and a lobbying group advocating for changes in the school lunch program. The group has ties to a company benefiting from the beef contracts."

As their revelations unfolded, my emotions intensified. We were starting to chip away at the walls of secrecy surrounding Centerville.

"We also reached out to some confidential sources," Holli added. "The rumors of discontent among a few town officials suggested that not everyone's aligned with Fredrick's interests."

Realizing that individuals in the system might be willing to challenge the status quo was a ray of light. Our conversation continued, each revelation sparking new avenues of inquiry, each connection a potential thread to unravel the truth. A flicker of hope ignited us, there may be fractures in the facade of Fredrick's influence.

Rebeccah's eyes alight. "So, what you're saying is that there's a possibility that Fredrick's grip on the community might not be unshakeable?"

Holli nodded, her expression infused with a spark of defiance. "We've heard allegations about discontent among business owners and town council members. It's like an undercurrent of resistance, a crack in the armor."

Samantha chimed in. "Those speculations led us to key figures who have felt the impact of Fredrick's influence and are tired of living under his shadow."

Samantha sipped her coffee before launching into her findings, her eyes alight with excitement as she unveiled them. "I delved into the virtual world of Centerville's digital footprints."

She recounted her journey, describing the cryptic online chatter she stumbled upon. "I found these forums and chat groups where people talk about the town's dynamics."

Holli chimed in, her analytical mind already connecting the dots. "Cryptic language, you said? Is it some code that allows them to communicate without raising suspicion?"

Samantha's fingers thumped across her laptop as she continued her digital journey. "Yes, and I uncovered a trail of deleted social media posts. It's as if some people are trying to erase any connection they might have to Fredrick or his business ventures."

Rebeccah's brows furrowed as she absorbed the details. "That's suspicious. It indicates that they're hiding something."

"Financial transactions. I found electronic trails of money exchanges between certain town officials and Fredrick's enterprises. This indicates financial ties, but the exact nature of these transactions is still unclear," Samantha said, her voice hinting at frustration.

Holli, her eyes narrowing in thought. "Could this be evidence? It would fit the pattern we've been uncovering."

"Every information is pointing in that direction," Samantha stated and shared her final discovery. Intrigue settled over the room. "I received anonymous tips and messages from individuals claiming insider information. They want to remain hidden but are willing to speak on what's happening behind closed doors."

Despite our best efforts, the list of names we hoped to compile remained frustratingly empty. The realization that we were grasping at shadows, without concrete evidence to implicate anyone, cast a veil of disappointment over our gathering. The weight of uncertainty bore down on us, and the room carried an air of subdued frustration.

Letting out a sigh, I mirrored the collective sentiment. "It's like trying to catch smoke with your bare hands," I remarked.

"Yeah," Samantha chimed in, a touch of exasperation coloring her words. "We have the parts, but they just won't fit together."

Glancing at the clock on the wall, I realized it was 7 p.m. The realization hit me like a jolt of electricity. "I need to go," I announced, a sense of urgency tingling at the edges of my consciousness. "I have a meeting with Aaron."

Samantha nudged my arm, a mischievous glint in her eye. "Off to meet your mysterious source, huh? Don't keep us in suspense—spill the details when you return."

Holli grinned and raised an eyebrow. "Yeah, spill all the juicy secrets. In the meantime, we'll be here unraveling our little mystery."

Chuckling at their teasing, it was a welcome distraction. "I promise I'll share everything when I get back," I assured them, already heading for the door.

"Good luck!" Rebeccah called after me, a note of encouragement in her voice.

My heart quickened as I scanned the tables, searching for Aaron's familiar face. Our eyes met as I reached the table, and Aaron's smile lit up. The corners of my lips lifted in response, and a sense of friendship settled between us.

"Hey," Aaron said, his voice warm and welcoming as he stood up.

I smiled, extending my hand for a handshake. "Thanks for meeting with me."

He took my hand, his grip firm yet gentle. "I've been looking forward to this."

Aaron gestured toward the empty chair across from him. "Please, have a seat. Can I get you anything? Coffee, tea?"

"I'll go for a herbal tea if there is any. Thank you." I responded.

"I have been worried about what might happen to you since you are investigating Fredrick," Aaron confessed, his voice tinged with genuine concern.

Offering a reassuring smile, though my curiosity piqued. "What could go wrong?"

Aaron responded. "Let's say, 'things'."

The weight of his unspoken words hung between us. A heavy silence that spoke volumes about the potential dangers that loomed on the horizon.

His eyes fixed on mine. "Breanna, you're committed to uncovering the truth but must prioritize your safety. This is treading on dangerous ground."

"I understand that."

"Consider being more discreet about your findings. Share your progress only with those you trust. Maybe reach out to someone with experience in dealing with these situations."

"You mean like hiring a private investigator?"

Aaron nodded. "Someone who can help gather information while keeping a lower profile. Your dedication is admirable, but your safety should come first."

"I appreciate the concern," I replied with a hint of gratitude. "We will consider it."

Aaron's glance bore attention. His words took on a hushed tone. "I will share crucial facts about Fredrick's misconduct. The names, dates, and events are all related, so our approach needs to be methodical."

Aaron's voice, concerned, broke through the silence. "Look at the school contracts. Fredrick manipulated the bidding process two years ago to ensure his ranch secured an exclusive beef supply contract with the local schools. To veil his ill-gotten gains, he orchestrated a series of kickbacks funneled through a shell company named GrangeProvision LLC. This shadow entity was the mastermind by an attorney named Zariyah Lehman."

My pen raced across the pages of my notebook, capturing names, dates, and intricate details. My mind raced to absorb the gravity of his words. I managed to inquire, my voice steady, "What about the timeline, Aaron?"

"Remember this key date: March 15th. That is when the initial bid was rigged," Aaron's words carried a firm resolve, guiding me through the convoluted path of deceitfulness. "From that moment onward, every quarter, there was a sinister current of tainted transactions."

My pen glided across the paper. The room buzzed with disbelief. The weight of our discoveries hung in the air. With each revelation, the complexity of the web deepened.

"The threads extended even into government contracts. There's a digital trail, electronic footprints leading from Lehman to several influential town council members." Leaning forward, he fixed his glance on me. "One name stands out above the rest – Councilman Rex Jones. The evidence suggests that he received these illicit payments on various dates, including June 9th and November 21st."

Rex Jones's involvement sent a jolt of shock. I exchanged a look with Aaron, the unspoken realization hanging heavy between us.

My heart raced. "How do these events tie everything together?"

"The moment arrived on July 5th with the mysterious fire that consumed one of Fredrick's smaller ranch buildings. It was a calculated act of arson aimed at obliterating any trace of the kickbacks. Councilman Jones orchestrated the blaze, enlisting the aid of a local troublemaker named Jake Barnes."

My hands quivered. "This- this is explosive, Aaron. The question is, how can we substantiate these claims?"

His stare held mine. "That's where your investigative prowess comes into play. You possess the connections, the resources, and the tenacity required to untangle this intricate web of corruption."

My admiration for Aaron deepened. I was drawn to his passion, skill in navigating the labrynth of misconduct, and willingness to venture into the realm of risk.

His words lingered in the air, and my curiosity burned brighter. "Aaron, where did you acquire these details? How did you piece together all of this?"

Aaron's response was gauged: "I have a concern for the cattle and the conditions in which they are raised. I have sources at all the ranches and in town who have gathered information for a while now."

The knowledge cast a somber backdrop to the final moments of our meeting.

Aaron's gentle yet sincere voice stirred something in me as he spoke, "Breanna, before we wrap up, I was wondering if... well, you might be interested in spending time together when all of this is over." His eyes held hope, and a tentative smile curved his lips.

With a composed but trembling heart, I returned his smile and replied, "I'd like that. Maybe after all this chaos, it would be a welcome change."

His smile broadened, genuine pleasure shining in his eyes. "Wonderful. I'll call or text you."

Stepping through my apartment door, the familiar sights and sounds surrounded me. The soft glow of lamplight painted a cozy ambiance, and the gentle hum of conversation filled the air. My heart swelled as I joined the friendly faces of Holli, Rebeccah, and Samantha, each radiating eagerness.

"Breanna, you're back!" Holli exclaimed, a delighted smile spreading across her face.

"Did you and Aaron uncover anything substantial?" Rebeccah chimed in, her eyes gleaming.

Settling onto the couch, I described how Aaron revealed a tangled web. He detailed the manipulation of school contracts, government facilities, and the orchestrated fire that destroyed evidence. I emphasized Councilman Rex Jones's pivotal role in this intricate scheme and how he used the local troublemaker Jake Barnes as an accomplice.

The room was full of shock and anger.

"We need to explore this," Holli said with resolve.

"We have to be cautious," Samantha added, her eyes darting between us. "With such players involved, our safety could be at risk."

A playful grin tugged at the corners of my lips as I continued, "Oh, and there's another tidbit Aaron shared with me."

Wonder sparkled in Samantha's eyes as she inquired, "Do tell."

I couldn't help but tease them a little, and my voice laced with a hint of excitement. "Aaron is interested in seeing me. He suggested we spend time together!"

Sharing the newfound detail, I felt excitement and mild embarrassment. Their reactions were a mix of surprised delight and playful teasing, as if this unexpected turn of events added a touch of lightheartedness. Rebeccah raised an eyebrow with a mischievous grin while Samantha's eyes twinkled with amusement. Always quick with a witty remark, Holli quipped, "Well, Breanna caught the attention of our informant."

Laughter filled the room, a welcome reprieve from the intensity of our discussions.

Chapter 8

Holli, Rebeccah, Samantha, and I gathered around the coffee table, forming a tight circle of collaboration. A tapestry of documents, notes, and photographs sprawled, with each piece like a puzzle. Our minds engaged, each synapse firing as we delved into the intricacies of Fredrick's web of deceit.

Emotions within me were like a whirlwind as I continued to plunge into the heart of our discoveries. Excitement surged through my veins. Beneath the surface, a current of apprehension tugged at me.

My mind was full of thoughts, memories of moments shared with Aaron intermingling with the threads of evidence collected. Aaron's earnest look, his voice unwavering and determined, as he unraveled the intricate tapestry of corruption.

Remembering how his words painted a vivid picture, each detail a brushstroke that brought the truth into sharp focus. Sitting across from him, my notebook open and pen poised to capture every revelation, was a memory. His presence had been a guiding light, illuminating the path I needed to follow. Amidst the echoes of those discussions with Aaron, our focus shifted back to the present.

Holli's furrowed brow was a tribute to her intense concentration. "Let's begin by dissecting the financial records," she suggested, her voice a steady anchor in the sea of information. "The payments to GrangeProvision LLC serve as a breadcrumb trail. We must follow it to its source, and the connections to the town officials implicated."

Rebeccah's eyes sparkled with fierce determination. "We should scrutinize his involvement in key decisions if Councilman Jones received them. Let's cross-reference the dates with significant events to uncover the hidden motives behind his actions."

Samantha's fingers were like a conductor's baton, orchestrating a symphony. "Let's not overlook the lobbying group ties. Their collaboration with Fredrick might be the linchpin in this elaborate scheme. We need to dive into their activities, trace their influence, and expose the extent of their manipulation."

"Exactly," I chimed in. "Let's not overlook the deleted social media posts. Those could be valuable clues. We should find out who was trying to erase their ties to Fredrick."

"I'll work on tracking down those posts and if we can recover any digital breadcrumbs. I will also explore the forums and chat groups where people discuss Fredrick's influence. There may be hidden messages or patterns we haven't discovered yet." Samantha stated.

Rebeccah locked eyes with me, her determination shining through. "It's on me to make contact with some of the key figures we've pinpointed in our research," she declared, her commitment resolute. "People like teacher Margaret Holman, Councilman Rex Jones, Oscar Turner—Trish Turner's brother—and Kim Wilson, a former GrangeProvision employee. These individuals might be willing to share their experiences. We can establish a connection built on trust. Their perspectives would be a crucial asset to our investigation."

"Are you planning to chat with everyone in a single day?" I quipped, raising an eyebrow at Rebeccah.

She chuckled, shaking her head. "Not likely. How about paying a visit during the week instead?"

I couldn't resist a playful retort. "Sure thing but be warned – early mornings are the name of the game! Count on me to lend a hand with those meetings."

We delved into the intricate mystery before us, each piece a potential breakthrough. A realization that our pursuit may lead us into the heart of a dangerous web of corruption.

"I'm also compiling a list of potential witnesses and informants. People having firsthand knowledge of Fredrick's dealings but have been too afraid to come forward."

"That's a smart approach," I acknowledged Holli's strategic thinking.

Rebeccah nodded. "With the new leads we're uncovering, we can strengthen our case against Fredrick. The more evidence we have, the harder it will be for him to evade the consequences."

A soft knock echoed through the apartment, interrupting our focused deliberations. Holli glanced at Rebeccah, her brow furrowing in surprise. With a glance in my direction, Samantha rose from her seat and made her way to the door.

The door creaked open, revealing a messenger standing on the threshold. The dim lighting of the hallway cast a subtle halo around his silhouette, giving him an almost ethereal appearance. In his gloved hand, he held a sealed envelope, the pristine paper exuding an air of importance.

"Delivery for Breanna Willis," the messenger announced, his expression impassive.

Samantha accepted it, curiosity flickering in her eyes. "Thank you," she replied, her voice cordial yet tinged with a hint of intrigue.

The door closed behind the messenger, and Samantha turned to face us, "It's a message from a courier," she explained.

I coursed through the room and took it from Samantha's hands. My heart raced as I gingerly broke the seal. The contents within were not what I expected – a sheet of paper with a series of random symbols and characters arranged in rows and columns.

"It's encrypted," I muttered. "It's coded."

The atmosphere shifted as we huddled around the coffee table again. Samantha's brows furrowed in concentration as she transcribed the symbols onto a digital document.

Holli nodded in agreement, "Let's look for recurring symbols, sequences that might indicate specific letters or words."

Samantha's fingers flew across her keyboard, her determination unwavering. "We can decipher this, leading us to valuable information."

The room was alive with hope. The seconds turned to minutes, and we worked in unison, poring over the cryptic message, searching for hidden meaning within the intricate arrangement of symbols.

With a sudden exclamation, Samantha pointed to a cluster of symbols that appeared more than others. "Look here – these patterns represent vowels. We treat the symbols in this sequence as consonants. We might be onto something."

We assigned letters to the symbols, and a revelation washed over us. Words began to emerge from the chaos, like hidden treasures unearthed through our collective effort. It began to transform into coherent sentences.

"I think we've got it," Holli declared. "It's from an anonymous source, someone who claims to have insider information about Fredrick's operations."

Rebeccah's eyes widened as the words took shape before us. "Beware of exposing the truth."

A palpable shift swept through the group, a current of concern darkening the once-determined atmosphere. The realization that we were stepping into uncharted territory, encountering new challenges and dangers, tempered the initial excitement.

I cleared my throat, my voice steady but tinged with caution. "Given this new development, maybe we should approach today with a bit of caution. Let's lay low for now – reach out to a few key figures we've identified and gather more information. It might be wise to stay here, spend more time researching, and ensure we're well-prepared for whatever lies ahead."

Rebeccah's gaze met mine. "Agreed. This meeting is important to gather facts before we take the next step."

Holli nodded, her analytical mind already processing the situation. "By connecting with our contacts and delving deeper into the research, we can fortify our position and make informed decisions moving forward."

Samantha tapped her fingers on the keyboard, and her eyes focused on the screen. "I can continue cracking the encryption further, just in case it holds additional information."

With a nod, we gathered our belongings, slipping notebooks, pens, and phones into our bags. The door creaked open, and we stepped into the hallway. The muted sounds of footsteps as we made our way down the corridor.

The vibrant sights of Centerville unfolded before us as we drove along the sun-dappled streets. A breeze rustled through the leaves of trees, carrying the refreshing scent of cut grass from a nearby park. Soon, we reached the café, its charming exterior inviting us to step inside. Rebeccah and I entered, and the rich aroma of coffee beans enveloped us in a warm embrace. The soft murmur of conversation filled the air, accompanied by the clinking of cups and saucers.

Our friend Chelsea, the café's barista, greeted us with a bright smile. "Hey, Breanna, Rebeccah! It has been a while! What can I get you today?"

Rebeccah's cheerful response met with a friendly laugh from Chelsea as she started preparing our orders. We waited. Chelsea leaned in conspiratorially, "You two won't believe the latest gossip that's been making the rounds in town. Small towns have a lot of stories."

Chelsea's voice dropped to a conspiratorial whisper as she shared the latest town gossip with me and Rebeccah. "There's talk of some changes coming to Centerville. The old factory on the outskirts of town? The one that's been abandoned for years?"

Rebeccah and I leaned closer to catch every detail.

"Well," Chelsea continued, her eyes sparkling with excitement, "rumor has it that a developer from the city has been sniffing around. Some folks say they want to buy the property and turn it into a luxury resort or a high-end shopping center."

Rebeccah's eyebrows shot up in surprise while my mind whirred with thoughts. "That's a massive transformation," I commented,

"Yeah," Chelsea replied with a knowing smile. "Some are excited about the potential boost to the local economy, but others are worried about the character of our town getting lost."

I nodded, understanding the sentiment all too well. "It sounds like this would stir up quite a debate."

Chelsea chuckled, pouring milk into a steaming cup of latte. "Oh, you have no idea. The town meetings have been livelier than ever."

Rebeccah signaled, a playful glint in her eyes. "Sounds like Centerville's getting drama."

Chelsea nodded. "Everyone has an opinion and is not shy about sharing it."

We couldn't help but share a knowing smile. Life in Centerville continued to buzz with its unique energy. I stepped outside and dialed Margaret Holman's number. The phone rang, the sound muffled by the gentle breeze that ruffled my hair. The call connected, and my heart quickened, knowing that each step we took brought us closer to unraveling the truth. The voice on the other end was warm and familiar, and as I explained my request.

"Margaret," I began, my voice blinking with eagerness and sincerity, "This is Breanna Willis. We are investigating influencing people in Centerville. I believe you have viewpoints that could be crucial to our cause. Would you meet me at the cafe in about half an hour?"

With a promise to meet, I ended the call and returned to the table where Rebeccah and Chelsea were talking. "What other stories have been circulating Centerville?" I couldn't help but speculate that the town held more secrets than just those connected to Fredrick's web of corruption.

Rebeccah's eyes lit up with a mischievous glint as she looked at Chelsea. "Oh, you wouldn't believe some of the tales people have been sharing," she replied, a playful grin tugging at the corners of her lips. "There's the mysterious case of the vanishing garden gnomes over on Elm Street – some folks think it's an elaborate prank war between neighbors."

Chelsea, her laughter ringing. "There's the legend of the 'Whispering Willow.' That old tree down by the river is said to grant wishes to those who can decipher its secret communication."

Our laughter subsided, and a sense of contentment settled over our small group. Rebeccah's eyes shined with amusement. Chelsea, her cheeks flushed, let out a contented sigh, her look drifting to the window as she lost herself in thought.

"I hate to break up the party," Chelsea began, her tone infused with regret, "but I've got to head out. There's a meeting at the community center that I promised to help set up for." Her words carried a touch of disappointment,

Rebeccah and I were grateful for our shared moments. "No worries, Chelsea," I reassured her, smiling. "Thank you for joining us and catching up. We'll have to do this again sometime soon."

Chelsea's lips curved into a genuine smile as she stood up, her chair scraping against the floor, her voice laced with sincerity. "If you ever need more town gossip or good company, I'll be right here."

Chelsea's departure left a gentle void in our midst. The soft sound of the cafe's doorbell signaled the entrance of a new presence. I turned toward the door; framed by the threshold stood a woman. The muted sunlight from outside cast a radiant halo around her silhouette. Her features obscured, before becoming clear, as she entered the cafe.

The cozy ambiance brightened with her presence. The soft murmur of conversations and the clinking of cups faded into the background, leaving only the hushed anticipation that filled the air. Her eyes scanned the room, and I waved to signal her to our table.

Feeling my pulse quicken. Her perspectives might be key to unraveling the mysteries gripping our town. I offered her a warm smile, inviting her to join us.

The soft shuffling of chairs and the gentle rustle of papers accompanied her approach. Rebeccah and I rose from our seats in unison, a silent gesture of welcome. Margaret's lips curved into a polite smile that belied the intrigue.

"Are you Breanna?" she asked, her voice melodic.

"Yes," I answered. "Are you Margaret?"

"I am," she responded. You mentioned you wanted to discuss something important?" Her words hung in the air, indicating her willingness to engage.

My eyes locked onto Margaret's as we took our seats, a silent exchange that conveyed the gravity of the situation. Rebeccah's presence beside me was both cautious and eager, her notepad ready to capture every detail that would escape her lips.

Rebeccah's soft yet insistent voice was a compass, steering the discussion into uncharted territory. "Margaret, thank you for meeting with us. We care about protecting the children and the quality of school lunches. Can you tell us more about the changes in the school lunch program and any potential connections to Fredrick?"

She took a steadying breath before sharing her observations: "Over the years of teaching, I discovered a pattern. A significant shift in the lunch program, but it didn't seem to favor Fredick's ranch."

I nodded, encouraging her to continue while my mind processed her words: "Go on, we're listening."

Her voice gained urgency as she leaned in, determination shining through. "There was a noticeable switch to processed foods from a local supplier, Alright Foods. The beef supply contract followed a similar trajectory, leaving me and some fellow teachers puzzled."

Rebeccah's pen crossed her notepad, capturing every detail as Margaret's words painted a clearer picture. "Did you overhear anything? Any conversation among the school board members?"

Margaret's eyes held irritation. "I did, but they spoke in code, hinting at 'favorable arrangements.' It seems they didn't want word to get back to Fredrick."

All veiled, yet the implications remained clear – more lay beneath the surface.

A swift exchange of glances between Rebeccah and me conveyed the weight of Margaret's revelations, casting a solemn atmosphere over our huddled discussion. The fragments we assembled were now unveiling crucial information. She stood and departed the cafe.

Excitement swirled with urgency as we contemplated sharing these revelations with the rest of our group. However, we needed to pursue another crucial piece to our puzzle: a discussion with Oscar Turner, Trish Turner's brother. The prospect of unraveling more layers of the mystery through his perspective compelled us to seek his observation.

Rebeccah and I shared a knowing nod, acknowledging the significance of our next step. We prepared to face the revelations in our upcoming discussion with him.

Reaching for my phone, my fingers tapped out a quick message to Holli, updating her about our conversation with Margaret. The text read:

"Hey Holli Just talked with Margaret Holman. Fascinating convo. Got some solid info. I will update you. Meeting Oscar next; fingers crossed for more details. "

With a satisfied nod, I sent the message and focused on the next task: reaching out to him. I dialed his number, my heart beating faster as I waited for him to answer. After a few rings, he picked up, his voice coming through the line.

"Hello?" he answered.

"Hi," I greeted, with a hint of eagerness. "It's Breanna Willis. Would you meet me at the cafe? We hope to ask about your perspective regarding your sister and Fredrick's ranch."

There was a moment of silence before he responded, his voice thoughtful. "I suppose I can make some time. The cafe, you said?"

"Yes, that's right," I confirmed a note of gratitude in my voice. "We'd appreciate your thoughts. Can we expect you in about an hour?"

Oscar agreed, and we exchanged a few more details before ending the call. My fingers tapped on the tabletop.

A gust of chilly air swept in as the door swung open, causing a shiver to run down my spine. Oscar stepped inside, his presence commanding attention. He scanned the room before gazing at us, his lips curving into a polite smile. The scraping of the chair against the tiled floor accompanied his approach as he joined us at the table.

As we discussed the matter hand, with a sip or two of the coffee, Oscar's eyes held a slight caution as we delved into Trish Turner's relationship with Fredrick. He recounted their interactions, painting a vivid picture of a sibling bond that had once been strong but frayed over the years. He hinted at Trish's growing distance and involvement in matters that raised his suspicions.

"There were times she'd receive calls and go off to talk in hushed tones," he revealed, his voice tinged with concern and frustration. "I overhear her mention 'contracts' and 'arrangements.' Something about 'ensuring things go' and 'ensuring the right people are on board.' It didn't make much sense then, but it stuck with me. I couldn't help but wonder what was so secretive. She is involved in something big, not wanting the rest of us to find out. I asked her about it later, but she said it was work. I grabbed her phone when she was not looking. The calls came from Fredrick."

"Do you have any proof?" I asked.

I don't have physical proof, but I can take some photos of her phone," he answered.

Oscar's departure from the cafe marked the end of a significant talk, and his words lingered in the air as he walked away. A mixture of concern and determination was etched on his face. The door closed behind him, and the atmosphere in the cafe shifted, leaving a sense of anticipation in its wake.

If Trish's actions and conversations were, as Oscar said, it would emphasize a deeper involvement with Fredrick's operations. Oscar's understandings hinted at a trail of potential secrets, each a breadcrumb leading us further down the path of corruption and deceit,

Rebeccah and I walked to the car. The world hummed with possibilities. Margaret's conversation injected fresh energy. The parts formed a clearer picture of the corruption seeping into the heart of Centerville.

Settling into the car seat, I took out my phone and typed a text message.

"Hi, Holli Just finished a revealing chat with Oscar. He gave us some intriguing insights into Trish's secretive phone calls but lacked physical proof. We're heading home to process it all. I will keep you posted. Take care! - Breanna"

Rebeccah and I stepped through the apartment doorway, our presence infused with urgency and anticipation. The atmosphere shifted as we entered, a ripple of intrigue passing through the room. Soft light illuminated the space, casting a warm and inviting glow that contrasted with the seriousness of the information we carried.

Holli and Samantha turned their attention from their tasks to us, their expressions transitioning from focused to expectant

"Hey," I greeted. "We're back."

Rebeccah's gaze swept across the room, intensity in her eyes. "Mind if we fill you in?"

We settled into seats, our attention directed towards them.

Samantha's voice was steady, a beacon of focus in the room. "So, what did Margaret and Oscar have to say?"

I took a moment to organize my thoughts. "Margaret had some eye-opening insights about the school lunch program. There's more to it than the quality. Financial records she received from a friend on the school board indicate something is going on."

A subtle furrow appeared on Holli's brow. "Fishy in what way?"

Rebeccah leaned forward. "Funds allocated for the lunch program are being diverted elsewhere. There's evidence of manipulated expenses and hidden transactions. It's a full-blown financial deception."

Samantha's lips tightened, a blend of frustration and anger coloring her features. "Using something as vital as the school lunch program for personal gain – that's a new shameful act."

Holli and Rebeccah exchanged glances, their eyes full of astonishment and concern. The weight of the information uncovered settled over them like a heavy fog, casting a shadow of unease in the room. The encrypted note and the convoluted money trail leading to the shell companies of GrangeProvision LLC revealed layers of complexity that were both daunting and intriguing.

Rebeccah's brows creased as she delved deeper into her thoughts. "We consider the encrypted note a clue. Then we must ask ourselves: who would go to such lengths to send us a message? Who knows about our investigation that would want to stop it?"

The question hung in the air, prompting a moment of introspection. The note's sender understood the investigation's intricacies and was aware of our focus on the school lunch program and the shell companies.

"Perhaps someone within Fredrick's circle?" Holli ventured, her expression uneasy. "It's possible that individuals within the organization aren't comfortable with what's happening."

Samantha leaned back in her chair, her thoughts aligning with Rebeccah's. "Maybe it's someone affected by the consequences of Fredrick's actions. Someone who's determined to bring their shady dealings to light."

The exchange continued, and Rebeccah's mind worked overtime, piecing together the puzzle while wrestling with the implications.

"The encrypted note is a challenge, but it's also a clue," Rebeccah said, her voice gaining a note of resolve. "We need to decode it to gain insights into who might be behind this and what they're trying to reveal. It's a puzzle waiting to be solved."

Samantha's fingers tapped against the table. "I never expected this puzzle to be this messy. It's like we're unraveling a web of secrets and deceit."

Holli considered the implications. "Whoever took the time to encrypt a message like that must have been desperate to keep their intentions hidden."

Samantha's voice held a tinge of frustration as she spoke. "I wish we had more elements of the puzzle. The money trail leads to dead ends and fake identities. It's like they've obscured the truth."

A spark of resolve ignited within Holli's eyes. "We've faced challenges. This won't be any different."

They gathered their belongings and prepared to leave. The atmosphere in the apartment was reluctant. I stood near the door, my expression mirroring the emotions that swirled within me. The prospect of saying goodbye remained a poignant reminder of the fleeting nature of such moments.

With their bags in hand, we exchanged hugs and smiles. Each hug held reluctance to let go and a desire to carry us forward. The door closed behind them, and I poured myself a glass of wine. The glass of wine I held embodied the serenity I needed. With each sip, I acknowledged that dawned would usher in fresh revelations, steering our journey into uncharted territory.

Chapter 9

The sensation of not being rushed tugged at the corners of my lips, urging them into a genuine smile. It was a day off for me. A rare moment in the middle of the week, but it was meant for rest by the station. I only needed to go in to have a meeting with Connie and John regarding the upcoming Town Hall. I moved with deliberate, unhurried motions. My tea, a mere companion for the commute, became a moment of indulgence. I took slow sips, savoring the warmth and rich aroma from the cup to my hands.

Beyond the window, people moved with a leisurely grace. Some walked their dogs, their furry companions stopping to sniff and explore with an equal lack of urgency. Others strolled hand in hand, engaged in conversations that carried on the breeze like fragments of melodies. I leaned against the windowsill, my gaze wandering across this slower, more deliberate world. The city transformed overnight, revealing a hidden side. The skyline, a backdrop to my busy mornings, now held a sense of majesty and calm, each building standing tall with its own story.

Leaving the window and focusing on the day ahead, I selected an outfit conveying professionalism and confidence while still being comfortable. I opted for a fitted blazer in a deep shade of blue, its tailored silhouette lending a touch of authority. Underneath, a simple white blouse provided a clean canvas for a delicate necklace with sentimental value.

Pairing the blazer and blouse with dark jeans, I slipped into ankle boots that would carry me through the day's endeavors. With a final glance in the mirror, I adjusted the blazer's lapels and ran a hand through my hair, ensuring a neat yet effortless appearance.

Stepping out into the morning, the city was now awake. The once-quiet streets transformed into a bustling thoroughfare, filled with a colorful tapestry of people going about their day.

Approaching the station, I couldn't help but appreciate the sights surrounding me. Storefronts came alive with merchandise displays, cafes offered the promise of a fresh start to the day, and snippets of conversations from passersby painted a mosaic of experiences. The architecture of the buildings stood tall against the sky, contributing to the neighborhood's distinctive character.

The intricate details adorning the exterior tell stories of bygone eras, proof of the city's rich history. The commuters flowed in and out, each individual absorbed in their thoughts.

The inside was alive with purpose. The clatter of footsteps on polished floors merged with the murmurs of conversation. I navigated the station's bustling corridors to Connie's office. Connie, the news producer, was sitting at her desk. Her blonde hair pulled back in a no-nonsense bun, and her dark-rimmed glasses perched on her nose gave her authority.

With a welcoming smile, she said, "Good morning. I'm glad we could meet before the Town Hall. There are a few logistics I wanted to go over to ensure we're well-prepared."

Just then, John walked into Connie's office. "Good morning, Connie, and good morning, Breanna. How are you today?"

"Fine," I answered.

John asked, "Did I miss anything?"

"No," Connie stated. We were beginning to discuss the logistics of the Town Hall and your responsibilities. First off, we're aiming for a lively and engaging atmosphere," Connie began, her eyes sparkling. "We'll have a diverse panel of experts, community leaders, and stakeholders, each bringing a unique perspective."

"John and you will serve as the moderators," she continued, her confidence in our abilities evident. "You'll open with an introduction, setting the tone for a respectful and insightful discussion."

I admired Connie's careful planning and commitment to creating an event that would illuminate the issues while encouraging a productive exchange of ideas.

"We'll also be taking questions from the audience," she added. "This is where your investigative skills will come in handy, Breanna. You will be able to have them dig deep into issues regarding our town."

I was excited about engaging and addressing their concerns. This would be an opportunity to bridge the gap between the public and the complexities of our investigation.

Connie concluded the presentation by highlighting the importance of maintaining a respectful and balanced atmosphere despite differing opinions. The event was shaping up as a platform for transparency. I was determined to fulfill my role as a moderator who would guide the conversation toward meaningful revelations.

The sun hung lower in the sky when I left, casting a warm golden hue across the city streets. Walking down the path, my steps brisk and purposeful, my thoughts consumed by the approaching event.

I walked, took out my phone, and composed a group text to Holli, Samantha, and Rebeccah:

Breanna: "Hey, everyone. I wanted to share some opinions with Connie. The Town Hall could be the perfect opportunity to stop Fredrick's manipulation. We'll have the audience and the chance to ask questions. I am looking forward to discussing our next steps."

Pressing send, a sense of resolve settled within me. This town meeting was our chance to bring our investigation to the forefront, gather the community's support, and confront Fredrick.

I waited for the responses.

Holli: "Yes!! This is what we needed!"

Samantha: "Wow, Breanna! This is huge. Count me in."

Rebeccah: "Interesting development. I'm all in. See you in a couple of days."

The support filled me, both empowering and reassuring. We were taking on an entity, challenging its deceit, and unraveling the manipulation. The thrill of the imminent Town Hall and the potential to expose Fredrick's actions were exciting yet terrifying.

Connie came out of the building. Her brisk pace and focused expression, told me she was on a mission. She stepped into the daylight. I approached her.

"Hey, Connie," I greeted, my tone severe but friendly. "Would you mind if I had your opinion on something?"

Connie paused, a hint of surprise flashing in her eyes before she nodded. "Sure, Breanna. What's on your mind?"

I motioned to a quieter corner nearby, away from the bustling activity of the station. I took a moment to collect my thoughts. The weight of our coming Town Hall and the revelations about Fredrick's actions pressed on me, but getting Connie's perspective would be valuable.

"I've been thinking about the Town Hall," I began, my voice measured. It's a big opportunity for us to expose Fredrick's dealings and bring their actions to the public's attention."

Connie's understanding was evident. "You're right."

Nodding, my gaze fixed on the ground before meeting her eyes again. "I value your journalistic views, Connie. What would be the most impactful way to present the information? How can we make sure that the community understands the extent of what's been happening?"

Connie thought as she considered my questions. "We need to focus on the human element – the stories of those affected by Fredrick's actions. Personal anecdotes can resonate more than just numbers and facts. It's about making it relatable and showing the real-world consequences."

Her words resonated with me, confirming the direction I had been leaning toward. "That makes a lot of sense. We must connect with people and make them invested in the outcome. We must be prepared for pushback from Fredrick – they won't go down without a fight."

We concluded our talk, and a sense of resolve settled over me. Connie's insight reaffirmed the path we were on. The Town Hall was an opportunity to catalyze change. I wanted to be part of that change.

A clang echoed from my phone. Glancing at the screen, I saw Aaron's name, and anticipation stirred. Opening the message, I could not hide my smile or the feelings I was beginning to have for this man.

Aaron: Hey, how's everything going? Are you holding up, okay?

Breanna: Yeah, I'm good. I'm just gearing up for the meeting. There is a lot to prepare for.

His swift reply came, carrying a warmth,

Aaron: I have no doubt you'll rock it. By the way, would you be up for a trip to the local winery? After all of this is over?

My heart skipped a beat at his invitation. Spending time with him was a chance to unwind and connect beyond the complexities of our respective roles.

Breanna: That sounds great! After all this, a winery trip sounds like the perfect decompression method. Count me in."

I hit the send button. The idea of sharing thoughts, laughter, and a glass of wine with Aaron was comforting.

The warmth of the sun's grip in the late afternoon sunlight contrasted with the cool breeze rustling through the city streets. The distant hum of traffic and the intermittent chatter of pedestrians filled the air, creating a comforting backdrop to my journey home. The walk to my apartment carried a sense of familiarity and routine.

My heels clicked against the pavement, like a metronome, as I passed by the quaint café where I stopped for a latte. The bookstore, with its inviting display of new releases, and the park, where children's laughter brought joy to the area.

The brick walls and the lined windows felt like an embrace - a haven - awaiting me after a hectic day at work. The lobby's lighting and the gentle elevator hum welcomed me back to a space with countless memories and the promise of tranquility.

A mixture of scents greeted me – the comforting aroma of the lavender-scented candle I had lit earlier and the faint traces of a meal I had prepared the night before. The ambiance of the living room casts a warm glow. Its soothing effect washed over me as I removed my shoes and set my bag down.

The plush couch invited me to sink into its cushions, and I obliged, allowing my weary muscles to relax. I closed my eyes and let the day's events wash over me – from anticipating the Town Hall to the stimulating conversation with Connie. The emotions stirred by our discussion lingered.

With a sigh, I opened my eyes and looked around the room, a sense of gratitude welling up within me. This space was more than just walls and furniture; it reflected my journey, a place where I could reflect, recharge, and find solace. The sights and sounds of my apartment—the glow of lamplight, the muffled sounds of the city outside—were a gentle reminder that I was where I needed to be.

Chapter 10

At the station, bustling activity filled the atmosphere. Colleagues hurried past, conversations buzzed, and the palpable energy of a newsroom in motion enclosed the space. My desk had been transformed with files, notes, and a scattering of coffee cups bearing witness to the flurry of work.

The constant hum provided a backdrop to my thoughts. Amidst it all, a familiar figure emerged – Rebeccah, navigating the room with a purposeful stride. My heart skipped a beat at the sight of her. With a quick smile, I left my desk and crossed the room to meet her. The impulse to connect was instinctual as we came face to face, and I wrapped her in a heartfelt hug. It was a surprise to see her here, and the warmth of the embrace conveyed my excitement.

"I wasn't expecting you until tonight," I admitted with a grin, releasing her but keeping our hands linked for a moment. Rebeccah's presence brought the warmth I needed.

Her eyes sparkled with eagerness. "I couldn't wait to start on the interviews. Time's of the essence with the Town Hall approaching."

I nodded. The event culminated our efforts, a crucial moment to expose and gather the community's support. The situation's urgency intensified, and Rebeccah's arrival only emphasized that.

"I'm glad you're here," I said, a sense of gratitude threading through my words.

Rebeccah's look met mine, an understanding passing between us. "It's time to dig deeper, to gather firsthand accounts and perspectives. With it drawing near, we must piece together the puzzle before we step onto that stage."

Her words resonated with me, reminding me of the event's significance. It was intended to confront and pave the way for policy change.

We discussed our plans, and the sounds of the newsroom faded into the background. The buzz of activity, the tapping of keyboards, and the muted conversations created a comforting backdrop to our conversation. Rebeccah's dedication to the cause mirrored my own.

"Should we begin with Councilman Jones?" I suggested.

Rebeccah's expression focused. "It sounds like a good place to start. Is city hall far from here?"

Taking a moment to assess the situation and the emotions swirling in me. "No, it's actually within walking distance. Parking can be a nightmare, so walking might be our best bet."

She nodded, agreeing to make the most of our time. I turned and led the way, Rebeccah stepping beside me. The streets stretched ahead. The sights and sounds of the city covered us as we walked. The thud of footsteps against the pavement, the distant honking of car horns, and the snippets of conversation from passersby created a setting that pulsed with life. Tall buildings rose on either side, casting long shadows as the sun descended.

"The city has a unique energy, doesn't it?" I remarked, my words carrying a touch of nostalgia."

We approached a crosswalk, waiting for the traffic signal to change. The pedestrian sounds and the distant honking of horns blended into a symphony of urban life. The movement shifted to the iconic white figure, and we stepped onto the pedestrian crossing, seamlessly weaving ourselves into the city's flow.

"I spoke to Councilman Jones's office earlier," I mentioned, "and they're expecting us. He's agreed to speak about his concerns over Fredrick's influence on local policies."

Rebeccah raised her eyebrows. "That's a strong lead. He's willing to speak, it might let us know the extent of Fredrick's manipulation."

We walked, and the imposing City Hall building came into view. The granite steps led to towering columns that supported the entrance, giving the structure an air of importance and authority.

"City Hall can be a maze," I warned, recalling the many times I navigated its corridors for research and interviews. "Inside, we'll find his office on the second floor."

It came into view, its architecture blending tradition and modernity. The imposing facade held a sense of significance, a place where decisions shaped the community's future. The flutter of flags in the breeze added a touch of color to the scene. The atmosphere shifted as we ascended the steps and entered the grand foyer. The echoes of our footsteps reverberated in the space, a reminder that our presence was a small yet significant part of the city's ongoing narrative.

We approached the directory and located Jones's office, following the signage through the corridor. The door bore a brass plaque with his name and title, symbolizing his responsibility in shaping the city's future. I raised my hand to knock, pausing to exchange a glance with Rebeccah. A pivotal moment to gather the information.

Sunlight streamed through large windows. He was a middle-aged man with salt-and-pepper hair and a severe demeanor, extending a welcoming hand as we entered.

"Good morning, Councilman Jones," I greeted, my tone respectful yet assertive. "I'm Breanna Willis, and this is Rebeccah Donaldson. We appreciate your decision to speak with us."

We sat at his desk. Rebeccah set up her recording equipment while I pulled out a notepad and pen. The room held its breath as if aware that this interview may unveil suppressed truths. He leaned back, his gaze thoughtful. "I appreciate your interest in my opinions. It's no secret that I've raised concerns regarding certain projects and proposals of Fredrick's during council meetings."

My interest piqued. "Could you delve deeper into those concerns? Which projects gave you pause?"

Councilman Jones's eyes reflected fatigue. "One project that caught my attention was redeveloping the old factory on the town's outskirts. Fredrick pitched it to rejuvenate our community, generate employment, and enhance tourism. Something felt amiss to me. The financial specifics remained vague, and there was a haste to greenlight it without thorough examination."

Rebeccah leaned forward, her pen poised over her notebook. "Did you speak up about these concerns during the council meetings?"

A rueful smile touched the councilman's lips. "I did, indeed. Questioning the lack of transparency, the potential impact on our environment, and the speed at which things move. My dissenting opinions are often ignored. It was as if the majority of the council had already made up their minds."

"Did you ever feel pressure from Fredrick or other members to change your stance?" Rebeccah inquired, her eyes keen.

He hesitated before answering. "Direct pressure? There were moments where I was sidelined or ignored, and I couldn't help but wonder if my resistance was costing me influence with the council."

I exchanged a glance with Rebeccah. The councilman's words hinted at a subtler form of power operating beneath the surface. It was the kind of pressure that went unnoticed yet wielded significant power.

Rebeccah's pen continued to move across her notebook. "Councilman, do you think Fredrick's influence extended beyond the meetings? Were there signs of their involvement in other aspects of the town?"

The councilman's expression shifted to a contemplative one. "I believe so. There were instances where Fredrick appeared to favor specific local businesses. These businesses received preferential treatment, which appeared linked to their connections with him. Contracts granted with minimal competition, and individuals who raised concerns about these decisions often faced obstacles."

"Did you ever attempt to investigate these connections further?" I asked, my curiosity growing.

He sighed, "I tried, but it was like unraveling a spider's web. The more I dug, the more I encountered dead ends and obstacles. It was frustrating, to say the least."

Rebeccah paused her pen as she looked up from her notes. "Your insights are invaluable to us. Your willingness to speak up, even when faced with resistance, is commendable."

He nodded. "Thank you. It's been a challenging journey, but I've always believed in doing what's right for our community."

Outside his office in the hallway, I leaned over to Rebeccah. "He's lying," I whispered. "You grilled him with questions, and I researched on my phone. He voted for it and left a public comment in the local paper, saying, 'This will benefit the town of Centerville for decades to come.' It's astounding how politicians still seem stuck in the past, oblivious to real-time fact-checking."

Rebeccah raised an eyebrow. "Impressive detective work. Looks like we've got a bona fide politician in the room."

We stepped out of city hall, and the sun's rays greeted us, casting a warm and hopeful light upon the world outside. The fresh air was a welcome contrast to the confines of the building, and I took a deep breath. The cool breeze carried away some of the tension that settled within me.

We strolled back to KBNR and climbed into my car. "I have an interview with Kim Wilson tomorrow, but perhaps she can meet with us today. Let me give her a call," I informed Rebeccah.

I dialed her number. "Hello?" she greeted after a few rings.

"Is this Kim Wilson?" I confirmed.

"Yes, speaking," she replied. "How can I assist you?"

"This is Breanna Willis. I know we were set to meet tomorrow, but I was wondering if you might be available this afternoon," I proposed.

"Of course, I can make time," Kim agreed.

"Great!" I exclaimed. "We'll be there in 30 minutes."

"Okay, I'll be waiting for you," Kim confirmed before we ended the call.

The residential neighborhood gave way to a quieter, more secluded area. Kim Wilson's address led us to a charming cul-de-sac lined with well-kept homes and blooming gardens. Pulling up in front of Kim's home, I parked the car and turned off the engine. We exchanged a moment before stepping onto the manicured lawn. The house was a two-story structure with a welcoming porch.

Kim Wilson, a former employee of GrangeProvision, was a potential key to unraveling the company's involvement in the town's affairs.

With a deep breath, I rang the doorbell. The moments that followed stretched as we waited for a response. The door swung open, revealing Kim Wilson herself. Her guarded yet searching eyes met ours as she stood in the doorway. The gentle rustle of leaves in the nearby trees and the distant hum of suburban life added to the ambiance, creating an almost surreal backdrop to our encounter.

"Ms. Wilson, thank you for agreeing to speak with us," I began, my tone respectful yet firm. "We're investigating certain matters that have come to our attention, and you may have critical insights."

Kim's view shifted between us, her guarded demeanor not faltering. "I appreciate your interest, but I need to understand the nature of your inquiry before proceeding."

Rebeccah's voice joined mine as we explained our connection to Fredrick's authority, the Town Hall event, and our goal of shedding light on the situation. Kim's eyes carried apprehension, curiosity, and a touch of vulnerability.

"As a former employee of GrangeProvision, we believe you might have insights helping us piece together the puzzle," Rebeccah added, her voice carrying a note of reassurance.

Kim's shoulders relaxed, her guarded expression giving way to a hint of contemplation. The warmth of the sunlight and the gentle breeze played against the backdrop of the weighty discussion unfolding.

"I understand your concerns and agree that aspects of my time at GrangeProvision need revealing," Kim spoke, her voice tinged with resolve and weariness. "I want to be clear that my involvement is not without risk. Some wouldn't take kindly to me speaking out."

We nodded, understanding it took courage for her to share her experiences.

"We respect your concerns, Ms. Wilson," I assured her. "You're willing to share your experiences, and we'll take every precaution to ensure your safety and privacy."

Sitting across from Kim in her cozy living room, the atmosphere was exciting. The lamps cast warm pools of light, creating an intimate setting that contrasted with the weighty subject of our conversation. Rebeccah and I sat poised, our notepads prepared to capture the details she was prepared to divulge. Kim's gaze remained steady.

Kim's voice recounted, "I once believed I was contributing to something significant – a company invested in the community and its future. Fredrick, the CEO, gave away himself as a visionary leader committed to advancement and creativity."

"As time went on, it became clear that Fredrick's vision was driven by more than just progress," Kim continued, her tone growing somber. "He wielded considerable control over the town council, including Councilman Rex Jones. Those who didn't align with his agenda were pushed aside or silenced."

"How were they silenced?" I inquired.

Her expression turned solemn as she replied, "Their presence around the office vanished."

Pressing further, my voice tinged with concern, "But do you know what might have happened to them?"

She leaned in, her words charged with a warning, "No, and you'd be wise not to investigate it, too."

Rebeccah's pen moved across her notepad, capturing her words as they unraveled the intricacies of Fredrick's manipulation. The air grew heavy with the realization that hidden agendas and power plays compromised the town's decision-making.

Kim's look held mine, "I came across documents, evidence of financial discrepancies and questionable deals. Fredrick used the company for personal gain, funneling funds into off-the-books accounts. I confronted him about it, and he threatened me, my job, reputation, everything."

The message she revealed was a damning revelation of corruption and manipulation. Kim spoke of the consequences she faced for challenging Fredrick's actions. I admired her courage.

"The consequences of speaking out against Fredrick were severe," Kim admitted, her voice tinged with resignation and defiance. "I chose to leave GrangeProvision to distance myself from the toxic power poisoning the town."

The warmth of the living room contrasted with the chilling realization that the town's well-being was being compromised by the person meant to guide its progress. We exposed his role as the puppeteer pulling the strings behind the scenes.

Our interview with Kim ended, and her vulnerability in sharing her experiences gave us a crucial piece of the puzzle. It was a deeper understanding of the impact and the lengths he would go to maintain his hold on power.

We thanked her for her willingness to share her insights. In my car, I wanted to share the information we had just learned with Holli and Samantha. Exhaling, I dialed Holli's number.

Holli's voice on the other end connected the call, her tone of inclination. "Hey, what's up?"

"Hey, Holli, let me go ahead and dial Samantha in on this call, too," I began, my voice steady but laced with what we learned.

"Hello," Samantha replied.

"Hi, we are all on the line," I replied. Rebeccah and I just had an intense conversation with Kim Wilson. She used to work at Grange-Provision and shared some important information about Fredrick's authority and the extent of his manipulation."

There was a brief pause on the line, the significance of my words sinking in. "Whoa, that's huge," Holli replied, "Tell me everything."

I summarized the key points of our interview. I sensed the tension on the call, the realization that we were at a crossroads in our investigation.

Samantha spoke up, "This changes everything. This is a valuable piece of information."

Holli chimed in, her tone resolute. "You're right, Samantha. It's time to put all the elements together."

"I agree," I affirmed, "We need to meet in person, put all the information on the table, and strategize our next steps. With the Town Hall meeting coming up, we have the perfect platform to expose Fredrick's actions."

Rebeccah and I concluded the three-way call with Holli and Samantha. We returned and found ourselves at the news station as the night grew darker. The quiet hum of the newsroom's equipment contrasted with the bustling energy that filled the space during the day. The dimmed lights cast a tranquil ambiance, and our footsteps echoed as we made our way to Rebeccah's car.

The journey from the news station to my apartment was a tandem of separate cars. I took the lead in my vehicle, and Rebeccah followed behind. The city's streets, alive with activity, were now bathed in the gentle glow of streetlights, creating a serene atmosphere.

My thoughts drifted between the intensity of the day's revelations and the path ahead. Glancing in the rearview mirror, Rebeccah's car trailing behind, our headlights cutting through the darkness in tandem. The sight of my apartment building was welcome, the familiar brick façade standing tall against the night sky. Pulling into the parking lot, I parked my car in its usual spot, followed by Rebeccah. Exiting our respective cars, Rebeccah and I exchanged a knowing look. Revelations and intensity filled the day. Now, the night promised a moment of reflection and rest.

My apartment had the familiar sights and sounds that defined my haven, the soft glow of lamplight and the comforting scent of a lavender-scented candle. Hours passed, marked by the intermittent sound of typing, the exchange of ideas, and the determined atmosphere that enveloped us. Rebeccah and I combed through the information we gathered, dissecting every detail and weaving the threads of insight into a cohesive narrative. The laptop screencast a soft radiance on our faces.

A knock on my apartment door broke the focused rhythm of our work. Rebecca and I looked at each other.

"Who can that be," I asked.

Rebeccah responded, "I don't know. We are not expecting anyone, are we?"

"No, but I better find out," I commented. "Who is it?" I asked through the door.

"It is your conscience speaking," a familiar voice said.

I opened the door smiling, and Holli and Samantha stood side by side.

"You are my conscience now?" I asked.

Samantha, her eyes focused and intent. "Yeah, we couldn't wait to get here."

With a welcoming smile, I stepped aside to let them in. Holli and Smantha had stopped and picked up dinner. The subtle scent of takeout food drifted through the air.

Rebeccah rose from her seat, and we gathered in a small circle. The room pulsed as I recounted the conversations with Councilman Jones and Kim Wilson. The implications of Fredrick's manipulation and the extent of his power were undeniable.

Holli broke the silence, her voice unwavering. "So, this is the web Fredrick spun. It's a complex puzzle, but now we have some key pieces."

"I've been diving into Margaret's story, and I've got some concerns," Holli shared, her tone reflecting apprehension. She continued, her voice steady but carrying a sense of urgency, "A subtle unease began to grow. It became clear that some of the parts in her narrative didn't quite align."

The emotions she invested in this research were evident, a blend of commitment and uncertainty. She took on the task of examining the threads of Margaret's story, weaving them into the larger tapestry of our investigation.

"I focused on the timeline of events. Discrepancies started emerging," Holli continued, "Margaret mentioned overhearing conversations among certain school board members, conversations that clear Fredrick in the corrupt activities we suspect. I cross-referenced those conversations with our own documented timeline of meetings and transactions. I discovered inconsistencies that raised doubts about the accuracy of her claims."

"Another red flag was the lack of concrete proof to back up her allegations," Holli continued, her voice steady. "Margaret hinted at financial transactions and connections between Fredrick and the changes to the school lunch program, but no tangible verification supports her claims. We've sought confirmation, and the absence of such evidence in Margaret's account is a significant inconsistency."

Holli's meticulous research peeled back layers of the narrative, exposing contradictions and gaps. Her pursuit made her question the authenticity of the information.

Samantha said, "It's likely that Margaret was attempting to lead us astray—to divert our focus from the real path. She played the role of a red herring, weaving a plausible narrative that led us away from the heart of the matter."

Holli's revelation sent a ripple of realization through the room.

Samantha added, "I scoured Margaret's social media," she began, her voice charged with intrigue, "I stumbled upon something rather intriguing. There were countless photos of her and Fredrick, not just casual poses, but ones as if they were dating."

Rebeccah's eyes narrowed as she pieced the puzzle together. "Ah, it's all falling into place now," Rebeccah concluded. "Margaret's eagerness to divert our attention was to shield him, to steer us away from him. We're unraveling her true motivations."

Samantha sat among us, and her knowledge was like a hidden gem. Samantha interjected, "Speaking of messages, I managed to break through the encryption of the anonymous message we received earlier."

The tension in the air was palpable as we gathered around, each of us holding our breath as Samantha's efforts bore fruit. Suddenly, the identity of the messenger, and the name appeared on the screen – Chris Fredrick.

"Why would Fredrick put his name out there? or is it coming from someone else?" I asked.

Samantha's voice held a hint of triumph as she contributed, "Although we do not have any hard evidence, I believe the note was from Fredrick himself. He is so arrogant. He never anticipated that we'd unravel the code. It fits the profile of someone who believes he is untouchable."

Samantha continued, "Oscar was on Fredrick's payroll. His task was to deceive us, fabricating accusations against Trish regarding school lunches and corruption. It is well documented through newspapers and video links that she would not have this point of view. These were matters she opposed during her school board election."

Samantha's breakthroughs marked a turning point in our investigation. We were able to connect the dots, laying bare the extent of Fredrick's manipulation and the depths he would plunge to maintain control. The encrypted message now revealed itself as a weapon turned against us.

Turning to Holli, I asked, "Do you believe we've gathered enough proof?"

Holli's response was strong. "Considering Samantha's findings, Aaron's revelations, and Kim's account, I'm confident that he and several others will soon be sporting orange jumpsuits."

With newfound clarity, we realized our efforts were about uncovering the facts and dismantling Fredrick's control over Centerville.

We parked the car at the police station.

I shut off the engine and turned to my friends. "We're in this together, every step of the way," I affirmed. "Thank you. It means everything to me."

We entered the precinct. The atmosphere was charged with urgency. We requested a meeting with Detective Ramirez. Moments later, we were escorted to a meeting room, where Detective Ramirez awaited us. We took the lead and laid out the proof we gathered—Kim's account and Aaron's revelations. The detective listened, jotting down notes as we recounted the intricacies of our investigation.

Holli detailed Margaret's inconsistencies, her meticulous research laying bare the doubts we uncovered in her story. Samantha's revelation about Oscar being on Fredrick's payroll, feeding us lies to frame Trish, added another layer of deception to the narrative.

We presented each piece of evidence. Detective Ramirez absorbed the details, his expressions shifting from intrigue to concern. With each passing minute, the gravity of our findings became apparent. The encrypted message was the linchpin that tied Fredrick to a web of deceit, manipulation, and personal interests. We finished presenting our facts. The silence in the room was deafening.

Detective Ramirez leaned forward, his gaze intense. "This is quite the revelation; you've brought forth substantial data. I'll need to consult my team and the district attorney before we proceed. Your efforts and diligence in bringing this to our attention are commendable."

Approaching Detective Ramirez, we expressed our intent to present our findings at the Town Hall meeting, confront Fredrick, and would need his assistance.

"I believe we can work on this together," he replied with a hint of reassurance, offering a playful wink before departing from the office.

We left the precinct, and relief came over us. The ball was now in the authorities' court to continue the investigation and possible charges. The magnitude of our research left us somber yet hopeful, knowing we had taken a crucial step toward uncovering the deception.

The confrontation with Fredrick was imminent, and the Town Hall meeting was now more than just a platform for discussion.

Chapter 11

F riday arrived, and Rebeccah, Holli, and Samantha had all committed to supporting each other at my apartment through the weekend. It allowed us to prepare for the Town Hall. The sun began to rise, the sky painted with hues of pink and gold.

The comforting scent of brewed tea surrounded the space. Preparing mugs for each of us, ensuring we started the day with a relaxing and refreshing tea. The sounds of the tea kettle and the clinking of mugs became a soothing backdrop to the excitement that filled the room.

Rebeccah, Holli, and Samantha arrived in the dining area individually. We exchanged warm greetings and smiles. Sitting around the coffee table, focusing on the tasks ahead.

The morning sunlight filtered through the curtains, casting a gentle glow over the room. The distant sounds of the city awakening, the birds chirping outside, and the hum of traffic created a sense of calm. The slight breeze rustled the leaves out, a reminder of the world beyond the walls of my apartment.

With our coffee mugs in hand, the morning sun casts a warm golden glow across our faces.

"A tremendous amount of progress last night with the conversations. We still need a strategy for the Town Hall on Tuesday," I remarked, breaking the silence. The rustling of papers and the occasional keyboard tap supported our discussion.

"We need people to attend and a little fiery, so the issues will make them want to attend," Holli's voice carried a sense of urgency, her eyes focused on the task at hand.

"So what angle do we take to ensure people will be there?" Rebeccah's was a challenge that required careful consideration. "The topic is the school board vote for beef contracts. School-age parents will attend. The topic is development. There will also be a limited crowd," Rebeccah continued, her brows furrowing in thought.

Samantha leaned forward, her voice filled with insight. "Why not do both? Leak enough information to spark their interest. It doesn't have to overwhelm them with all the details – we can save those for the meeting."

The room fell into contemplative silence as we absorbed Samantha's suggestion. The gentle breeze wafted through the open window and carried the weight of our shared thoughts.

"Who will leak the information?" Holli's practical question broke the silence, the challenge of finding the right messenger hanging in the air.

A spark of enthusiasm ignited within me as an idea formed. "We'll have John to do it," I said, a sense of confidence in my voice. "Remember, he's not one to shy away from unsolicited news. He'll leak the facts for us."

The scent of the tea lingered in the air as we hatched our plan. The plan promised a larger crowd and Fredrick's presence in the front row.

"Alright, ladies, I need to disappear for a bit and get ready," I announced with a mischievous grin. "I've got something up my sleeve boosting our strategy."

Moments later, I emerged, and a combined gasp escaped their lips as they caught sight of my outfit. I stood before them, exuding a combination of confidence and elegance. A tailored blazer with a deep emerald hue accentuated my eyes, and fitted black slacks added a touch of sophistication. A statement necklace completed the ensemble, adding a pop of sparkle, and my hair was in a stylish updo, highlighting poise.

"Wow, you look amazing!" Holli exclaimed.

Rebeccah's eyes lit up in agreement. "Stunning! That outfit is going to turn heads for sure."

Samantha nodded in support. "Bre, you're going to command attention. Your style is the perfect blend of professionalism and confidence."

My cheeks tinged with a faint blush as she soaked in their reactions. "Thanks, guys. I wanted to ensure I dressed to impress.

With a nod of affirmation, I headed toward the door.

The city streets I walked about countless times were now dear to my heart as my very soul. Entering the station, I walked through the familiar corridors, greeted by the hum of activity that defined the newsroom. In these halls, stories were revealed, investigations pursued, and the truth brought to light. Amidst the bustling atmosphere, I crossed paths with Jackie, the talented makeup artist whose expertise helped create my onscreen appearance.

Jackie's warm smile greeted me, and we exchanged a brief conversation. Her positive energy was a reassuring presence, a reminder of the dedicated professionals who played a role behind the scenes. I continued my journey to the studio, my heart pounding with excitement and focus.

Stepping onto the set, I recognized the familiar sights and sounds—the poised cameras, the lights casting their radiant glow, and the polished professionalism defining our broadcasts. John, my co-anchor, was already present. His calm demeanor and confident stance testify to his years of experience in the field.

The chemistry between John and I was a dynamic of common admiration. We shared the screen for a month, and our ability to seamlessly transition between scripted segments and unscripted commentary reflected our rapport.

The broadcast commenced, and he and I exchanged dialogue, our words flowing as we addressed the day's headlines. Our onscreen presence resulted from careful preparation and a shared commitment to delivering accurate and impactful news to our viewers. The professionalism we exhibited on camera was a culmination of years of dedication and a deep understanding of the responsibility that came with our roles.

"Hey," I began, leaning in with urgency. "Have you caught wind of the news? Fredrick's company is on the verge of winning the contract again. The concern is they've agreed to use—there are murmurs about the nutritional quality and the meat sourcing."

He raised an eyebrow, "Is that so? Tell me, what else have you dug up in your investigation?"

Shaking my head, my expression somber. "Not much more for now. What's alarming is the potential impact of the factory development."

John's features tightened, his concern evident. "That's a situation we can't ignore. We've got to address this head-on at the meeting on Tuesday. I'll loop in Connie and have this on the agenda."

Nodding in agreement, I let out a small sigh. "I think that's a solid plan of action. The community needs to discuss these issues and push for transparency."

Manipulating John wasn't a tactic I relished, but sometimes, getting the wheels in motion was necessary. News traveled fast in this town, and if I wanted to ensure the proper discussions, I needed to light the fuse.

Leaving the station behind, I returned home to my friends. I entered my apartment and found Holli, Samantha, and Rebeccah huddled around the table, their heads bent over a stack of papers.

"Breanna, you're back just in time," Holli said, looking up with a grin. "We've uncovered some new evidence."

They began sharing the details, and the room came alive with energy. The facts fell into place, revealing a clearer picture. Our efforts paid off, and the truth emerged. The meeting with the needed data was just around the corner.

Saturday came with a sense of purpose. Our plans were set, and the event was drawing closer. Visiting the local farmer's market was a chance to clear our minds and immerse ourselves in the community.

I looked around at my friends, each dressed in her unique style that reflected her personality and mood. Holli opted for a comfortable yet stylish ensemble, wearing a flowy bohemian top paired with jeans and a hat. Samantha exuded professionalism and confidence in a tailored blazer and dress pants, with a hint of her signature bold accessories. Rebeccah embraced a casual chic look, donning a vintage graphic tee, denim shorts, and a pair of worn-in sneakers.

Arriving at the market, the sights and sounds enveloped us in a sensory feast. The vibrant colors of fresh produce, handmade crafts, and fragrant flowers created a kaleidoscope of beauty. The bustling energy of vendors and shoppers mingled with the gentle hum of conversation, creating a symphony of community connection.

Holli's eyes lit up as she spotted a stall overflowing with organic vegetables and fruits. She couldn't resist picking up a basket of ripe strawberries, her excitement evident as she chatted with the farmer about sustainable farming practices. Samantha's gaze swept over the various stalls, her attention drawn to the artisanal cheeses and local honey. The intellectual curiosity that defined her was now captivated by the intricate flavors and stories behind each product.

Rebeccah went to a booth featuring handmade jewelry crafted from repurposed materials. She initiated a conversation with the artisan, and her genuine interest in the creative process was evident as she examined each piece. The aromas mingled with baked bread, spices, and the earthy scent of plants. Laughter and friendly exchanges created a tapestry of community connections.

Engaging in cheerful conversations with local vendors and fellow shoppers. It was as if the shared anticipation of the Town Hall renewed the air.

Selecting a few fresh vegetables and exchanging friendly banter with a farmer, The topic of the meeting was on everyone's lips. A sense of excitement and curiosity permeated the conversations. People were interested in being part of the discussion, eager to voice their concerns and opinions about the town's future.

"Breanna, are you going to be at the meeting on Tuesday?" a friendly face inquired as I browsed a table of handmade soaps. The question resonated with others nearby, I found myself surrounded by a small group of people, all curious about my involvement.

Smiling, I nodded and replied, "I will attend. John and I are hosting it."

I felt satisfied. Our plan to create awareness and interest in the event was working.

Continuing to mingle and chat with the marketgoers, I found myself face-to-face with Elias. His warm smile and easy demeanor put me at ease as we exchanged pleasantries.

"Breanna, it's good to see you again," Elias greeted, his eyes reflecting a warmth. "I've heard about the upcoming Town Hall. You and your friends are stirring up some buzz."

I chuckled, the realization our actions were indeed generating attention sinking in. "Yes, it's been quite a journey."

Our talk flowed. Elias's genuine interest in the town's well-being was evident.

The gentle hum of the car's engine provided a soothing backdrop. My friends and I recounted the friendly encounters at the market and the interest people showed. With our bags of fresh produce beside us, the car felt cozy and filled with positive energy.

We turned our attention to the Town Hall meeting plans at my apartment. This pivotal event had the potential to expose Fredrick's manipulation and inspire the community to demand change.

I chimed. "Now, we need to focus on the meeting itself."

Holli's expression grew thoughtful as she spoke up. "We also need to consider our safety. Confronting Fredrick in a public forum like the Town Hall could have consequences. We need to prepare for any potential backlash."

Her concern reminded us of the risks we took, the delicate line between exposing the truth and safeguarding ourselves. The room grew quiet as the weight of Holli's words settled in.

As the evening progressed, our discussion shifted to the logistics of the upcoming event. We discussed the agenda, the speakers, and the details that would ensure a successful event. Our collective efforts focused on the common goal of inspiring change.

Chapter 12

Tuesday afternoon arrived, and with it, a swirl of heightened emotions. The town's atmosphere charged as if the air crackled. The meeting was imminent, and my heart racing as the minutes ticked. The sunbathed the town square in a warm light, creating a sense of calm that contrasted with the intensity of the upcoming event.

A knock on the door signaled my friends' arrival. Rebeccah was the first to step in, her confident stride accentuated by a tailored blazer, crisp white blouse, and sleek black pants. Her gaze met mine. "We're ready for this," her expression said. Holli followed, her bohemian style interwoven with sophistication. A flowing green top and well-fitted jeans displayed her unique personality. Her eyes shimmered with excitement and nerves, and her fingers fiddled with her hat. Samantha entered the room last, her professional attire reflecting her analytical mindset. A navy blazer and statement necklace highlighted her confidence, while her steady gaze conveyed readiness."

Gathering in the living room, our conversations blended strategy discussions and words of encouragement. We reaffirmed our key points, making sure we were prepared to address any doubts that might arise.

"The evidence is overwhelming. The research is solid," I spoke.

The clock's ticking underscored our discussions, each passing minute bringing us closer to the Town Hall meeting. The trip to City Hall was a blend of excitement and tension. An emotional journey mirrored the significance of the Town Hall meeting. The streets buzzed with energy as if the entire town was converging on this pivotal moment. The sun set, casting a warm, amber glow over the city.

My friends and I made our way towards City Hall. Seeing people entering from all directions was awe-inspiring. The air was alive with snippets of conversations, laughter, and occasional hushed exchanges.

The exterior of City Hall was in soft light, its grandeur illuminated against the backdrop of the night sky. A line had already formed, stretching down the street, a diverse array of people wanting a seat at the meeting that would shape the town's future. The crowd's murmurs created a hum of energy as if the building was absorbing the anticipation hanging in the air.

Hope radiated from those who stood shoulder to shoulder. The sights were a spectrum of faces, ages, and backgrounds. An accurate representation of our community coming together. The occasional hushed exchange about the issues bringing us here punctuated the sounds.

The line moved slowly forward, inching closer to the entrance of City Hall. The city lights glowed, casting a gentle glow that added to our unity.

We entered the grand foyer of City Hall, and the sheer magnitude of the gathering hit me. The vast space was filled with faces. The meeting room was a symphony of colors as eager people filled the rows of chairs. The stage and the town emblem were a visual reminder of the significance of this space.

Taking our places, the room buzzed with vigor. Witnessing so many faces filled me with pride and a sense of responsibility.

Aaron's information about who was involved and the timeline provided the breakthrough we needed, the missing fragment that set our plan into motion. Amidst the crowd, we waited for the Town Hall meeting to start, and my thoughts drifted to him.

With a deep breath, I scanned the room, seeking Aaron's familiar face. He remained elusive in the vast crowd.

The event began, and I took my place at the front of the room alongside John, my co-anchor. Seeing the podium and the sea of expectant faces filled me with excitement and nervousness. The room was calm as he and I prepared to moderate the meeting.

"Good evening, ladies and gentlemen," I began, my voice carrying through the microphone. "Thank you all for being here tonight.

"Our speakers tonight come with a wealth of knowledge and a commitment to our town's well-being," John added, his voice resonating with authority. We invite you to listen, ask questions, and engage in a meaningful dialogue."

He and I stepped back, yielding the spotlight to our first speaker, and a sense of purpose settled over me. The Town Hall meeting was now in full swing, and I was ready to moderate with the same dedication which fueled our journey thus far. The room was alive with conversations. The stage adorned with microphones would amplify the voices of those who came.

Oliver Mitchell, a town business owner, addressed the crowd, emphasizing the importance of transparency and accountability. A dedicated social worker, Ingrid Newman, with her voice filled with empathy, spoke about the pressing social needs within our city, urging us to come together and make a difference. Daniel Davis, a concerned citizen of Centerville, captivated the audience with his insights into involvement and grassroots movements. He discussed the pivotal role local officials play in bringing about meaningful change.

The speakers all had a chance to speak. They fielded questions, and the audience was engaged, and some even applauded as they heard about the ideas for their town. It was turning into a night designed for the goal.

My friends and I took the stage to speak. I stepped forward to the microphone, my heart pounding. I looked at the crowd, recognizing familiar faces and unfamiliar ones.

"Good evening," I began, my voice carrying confidence. "To those who may not know me, I'm Breanna Willis, new to our town. In my short time here, I've had the privilege of speaking with many of you. I have gained insights into the fabric of our town."

A wave of nods and murmurs of acknowledgment rippled through the audience. Their attention was unwavering, their curiosity piqued by my words.

"I've come to realize our community comprises hardworking individuals who care about the place we call home," I continued, gazing over the crowd. "I've also encountered stories suggesting practices might not always be fair or ethical."

The rustling of papers and shifting seats created a subtle backdrop to my words. This was a sign people were listening, eager to hear what I had to say.

"I believe in the power of truth and justice," I emphasized, my tone firm. "That's why I've been researching certain practices that have raised concerns. We are prepared tonight to expose these matters."

The sight of the auditorium, filled with diverse people, was a witness to the community's investment in this event. The soft lighting cast a warm glow over the room, creating a severe and inviting atmosphere. The hushed murmurs and the occasional rustle of papers added to the charged ambiance, underscoring the gravity of the situation. Taking a deep breath, I stepped forward to the microphone, my heart beating with nerves and resolve. I looked at the sea of faces.

"Ladies and gentlemen," I began, my voice steady. "My friends and I have dedicated our time and efforts to investigate several issues that have cast a shadow over our town. These issues, some of which date back five years, have raised ethical concerns."

The crowd's attention was unwavering, their expressions of curiosity. "We intend to address these concerns," I stated. "We must ask some difficult questions. Mr. Fredrick."

I directed my gaze toward Fredrick, seated in the audience. He kept a guarded expression, and a trace of unease flickered in his eyes.

"Mr. Fredrick, is it true you were involved with teacher Margaret Holman and coerced her into providing us false details about your company and its proceedings?" I asked, my voice clear and unwavering. "This information was to protect you because you are both involved. Please understand that more important questions need answers."

Rebeccah stepped forward, her voice strong and resolute. "Did you pressure Trish Tanner to vote against her conscience and favor your company's beef contract with the schools? Did you threaten her with false charges against her brother, Oscar, if she did not comply? Please refrain from answering this question at this moment. There is a mountain of forensic evidence, including emails and bank records. Hold off on answering the question. There is still more."

A ripple of murmurs and gasps spread through the room, the gravity of Rebeccah's words sinking in. Fredrick's face showed a combination of shock and uneasiness.

Holli's turn to address the room, her gaze unwaveringly fixed on Fredrick. "Your attorney, Zariyah Lehman, is absent. He is usually at your side, but not tonight. The authorities have apprehended him in connection with shell company wire transfers traced back to a business registered under your name, GrangeProvision, LLC. Our investigation highlighted this information, substantiated by an anonymous source and bank records. Did you know anything about this? You needn't respond to this inquiry at this time, either."

The room hung heavy with silence as the attendees stirred. The truth had been laid bare, and the undeniable impact of our findings reverberated through the room.

Samantha's voice sliced through the air, her tone as sharp as a blade. "Mr. Fredrick, take a look around," she said. "Do you see Councilman Jones anywhere?" Her eyes locked onto his, piercing like daggers. "We've gone deep into his dealings, as well. The records speak for themselves. GrangeProvision, LLC funneled hefty sums into his pockets and the inferno that razed your property? It was his handiwork, orchestrated to obliterate any traces of guilt. Jake Barnes, brave as ever, came forward with his testimony. Jones hoped the flames would cleanse his sins, but the digital breadcrumbs remain."

"It turns out. Councilman Jones received a sweet kickback for greasing the wheels on the new development out on the town's fringes at the old factory. He's probably sharing a cozy cell with Lehman by now. Witnesses and a trail of digital footprints don't leave much room for doubt. So, would you care to enlighten us about your cozy financial connection with him? Did you have anything to do with this? On second thought, don't bother answering."

I stepped closer to the microphone, my heart pounding. The auditorium seemed to pulse with charged energy.

"Does the name Joyce Black ring any bell?" My voice crackled with an emotional plea for justice. "She dug into your corporate empire and vanished. Our exhaustive research unveiled a grim truth – her lifeless body was discovered a hundred miles from where we sit now. Digital forensics traced a damning trail of emails between you and her. Were you involved with this? You needn't trouble yourself responding to that question, either."

Pausing for a breath, I looked at my companions. Our revelations' gravity cast a spell over the room, capturing everyone's attention. In the charged silence, the weight of unanswered questions hung heavy, a palpable force bridged the gap between us and the audience.

"All the questions we asked tonight, Mr. Friedrick, only have one answer: yes. We have shared your answers. One question demands your response tonight," I continued, my voice unwavering. Do you happen to know the name of a reputable attorney? You're going to need one."

The tension mounted, the auditorium doors swung open, and the local law enforcement entered, moving with a purpose marked the end of Fredrick's unchecked reign. The auditorium erupted into a cacophony of emotions as the local law enforcement took Fredrick into custody. Some attendees cheered, their voices ringing with relief and triumph.

With Fredrick's departure, the atmosphere in the auditorium began to shift. Conversations erupted among the attendees, voices rising to fill the space as people processed the shocking information they had just witnessed. Whispers of disbelief and anger mingled with expressions of gratitude for our investigation.

Taking a deep breath, I stepped forward to the microphone again, my voice cutting through as the room quieted. "Ladies and gentlemen," I began, "we understand this is a lot to take in." The crowd's attention shifted towards me, their eyes locked on the figure at the front of the room. The emotions in the auditorium ranged from shock to resolve.

John, my co-anchor, joined me at the podium. His presence bridges our roles as journalists and the people we serve. "Tonight," he added, "marks a turning point for our town. The events that have unfolded here underscore the importance of community. We must work together to build a better future." John and I stood side by side. The crowd's attention remained riveted on us, and the words resonated with those present.

With a glance at my friends, I nodded to John. Together, we stepped away from the podium, leaving the auditorium in transition.

At my apartment, we turned on the TV to KBNR's local news and saw how the coverage played out. It displayed images of Fredrick taken into custody, captured the reactions of the Town Hall attendees, and featured interviews. The news anchor's voice encapsulated what just transpired.

We settled onto the sofa, each holding a glass of wine—a quiet gesture of celebration and solidarity. The soft glow of the room created an atmosphere of warmth and camaraderie. Watching the news coverage, there was a swell of fulfillment as our efforts were broadcasted. The weight of my roles as a journalist, a friend, and a community member felt more profound than ever. Pride and humility mingled within me, knowing our actions contributed to revealing the truth.

My heart skipped a beat as the familiar buzz of my phone indicated a new text message. It was Aaron. The emotions coursing through me intensified as I read his message.

"Breanna, I just saw the news coverage. You did it! I'm so proud of you."

Tears welled up in my eyes as I absorbed his words. I typed out my reply.

"Thank you, Aaron. Your information was the breakthrough we needed. We couldn't have done it without you."

Reading Aaron's message, I felt exhilarated. The words "See you on Saturday for the winery visit" promised shared moments and a future filled with camaraderie.

Responding with a quick "Definitely," I couldn't help but smile.

Chapter 13

Saturday arrived, carrying with it a sense of anticipation that was both familiar and exciting. The morning unfolded with a race as the soft sunlight filtered through the curtains, casting a glow across the room. The air had the delicate aroma of steeping tea leaves wafting from the cup on the table.

Sitting by the window, cradling a steaming cup. The steam spiraled upwards, bringing a comforting blend of earthiness and warmth. The delicate notes of chamomile and lavender infused the air, creating an atmosphere of calm anticipation.

Outside, the world awakened with a soft murmur. The rustling of leaves, touched by a light breeze, accompanied the distant song of birds as they welcomed the day. The garden, kissed by morning dew, exuded a fresh and vibrant scent.

I took a sip. The taste reflected the morning itself and the realization of what lay ahead. The cup between my hands radiated comfort as if holding a piece of the morning's embrace within it.

A quiet contentment in this moment of solitude, a sense of being connected to the world outside while relishing the intimacy of my thoughts. The day stretched before me, a canvas waiting for experiences, and the tea provided a soothing companion for the journey.

I thought about how our conversations might flow, tracing the contours of our interests and the stories exchanged. The soft curve of his smile played in my mind like a cherished melody. I envisioned the laughter that might bubble between us. Imagining the cadence of his voice, I wondered how it would blend with mine in the space between words, forming a rhythm that was ours.

Beyond the surface, my thoughts delved more, exploring vulnerability. I wondered if he, too, experienced the flutter of nerves, if his heart danced with the same mixture of uncertainty and excitement. Pondering the stories he had not shared, the experiences that shaped him, and the dreams that kindled his passions. Amidst these musings, I reflected on the unspoken chemistry, the uncharted territory where two souls might meet and intertwine. Would there be moments of silence that spoke volumes? Would our eyes meet, carrying messages words couldn't convey?

With my intimate thoughts lingering like a whisper, I set aside my cup of tea and concentrated on getting ready for the date with Aaron. The anticipation reached a crescendo, and the time had come to transform those dreams into reality.

I settled on a sundress that flowed around me. Its floral pattern reflected the vibrant surroundings in which I was about to immerse myself. The fabric was cool against my skin as I slipped into it, and the dress's bodice embraced me with a hug.

The delicate straps offered a hint of femininity suited for the occasion. I fastened a small necklace around my neck, the pendant nestled above the neckline, a subtle accent catching the sunlight as if it held a secret shimmer. Securing a thin belt around my waist, adding a touch of definition to the ensemble.

With a final glance in the mirror, I saw the dress complimented my features—how the hues highlighted my eyes and the silhouette highlighted my figure. Like a canvas, its colors and design expressed not my style but the spirit of the moment—a canvas ready to be painted with the emotions of the evening ahead.

I approached my car, its metallic surface shimmering under the late afternoon sun. The faint breeze carried the scent of blooming flowers, mingling with the excitement, quickening my pulse. Opening the door, I settled into the driver's seat, the familiar comfort of the leather embracing me like a reassuring hug. The wind tousled my hair as I drove, carrying away any lingering doubts. The sunlight filtered through the trees, dappling the road with an embrace, mirrored my feelings.

With the vineyard's entrance in sight, my heart quickened. The sight of the vineyard's entrance came into view, marked by an elegant wrought-iron gate that welcomed visitors. Beyond the gate, rows of grapevines stood in neat alignment, their leaves catching the sunlight in a dance of greens and golds. The tranquil beauty of the scene was a soothing balm. Reminder moments of respite were as vital as moments of action. I parked the car, the engine's growl tapering into a hushed stillness.

The moment arrived—the culmination of thoughts and preparations led me to this point. Stepping onto the vineyard grounds, the crunch of gravel underfoot echoed through the air. Stone pathways led the way, and wooden barrels added a touch of authenticity to the surroundings. The distant hum of conversation and the soft clinking of glasses hinted at other visitors' presence, but the vineyard's expanse allowed for pockets of solitude.

My fingers brushed against the petals of a nearby rose, its softness a tactile reassurance. I closed my eyes, allowing the morning's serenity to wash over me. The sound of birdsong filled the air, punctuating the stillness with a melody resonated with my heartbeat. With a final deep breath, I focused on the day's plan. The thought of spending time together, away from the intensity of recent events, brought a sense of tranquility that was both welcome and grounding.

A sense of excitement rose within me as I caught sight of Aaron. He stood beneath the shade of a sprawling tree, a figure easing amidst the vineyard's beauty. His smile was genuine. Our eyes met, and a wave of comfort settled over me.

Aaron's smile put me at ease. Our eyes met, and a comforting wave washed over me, vanishing my nervousness.

"Breanna," he greeted, his voice a soothing melody carried over the breeze. "You look stunning."

The compliment brought a subtle blush to my cheeks, and I offered a grateful smile in return. "Thank you, Aaron. You're not looking too bad yourself."

We wandered through the vineyard, and Aaron and I discussed anecdotes and stories that depicted our lives. It created an atmosphere of genuine connection and laughter. I began by telling him about a cooking mishap involving a failed attempt at baking a cake. "So there I was, covered in flour, trying to salvage what was supposed to be a masterpiece," I recounted, grinning. It turned into a flour explosion more than anything else!"

Aaron chuckled, his eyes sparkling with amusement. "Oh, I can relate. I tried to make pancakes and ended up with something that resembled more of a map of the world than actual pancakes. My family still teases me about it."

We both laughed, and our easy camaraderie grew. "Well, at least we can both appreciate the beauty of culinary adventures, even if they don't always go as planned," I said, nudging him.

He nodded, his smile warm. "It's all about the journey, right?"

Our conversation ventured into childhood dreams, and Aaron disclosed, "You know when I was a kid, I had a connection with animals. I spent an entire summer trying to communicate with squirrels in the park."

Laughing, imagining a young Aaron trying to converse with squirrels. "Oh, that's amazing! Did they ever respond?"

He grinned. "Well, I thought they did, but looking back, I'm pretty sure they were doing their usual squirrel things."

Listening to Aaron's stories, a warmth radiated from within. His laughter was contagious, and his anecdotes drew me into a world where humor and vulnerability coexisted. With each tale he recounted, I connected not with the words but with the emotions beneath.

I couldn't help but see the playfulness in his eyes, a glimpse into his willingness to embrace life's imperfections. It painted a picture of a young boy with an adventurous spirit and an endearing belief in the extraordinary.

With each story, I sensed the layers of formality and nervousness often accompanied by first dates slowly peel away, revealing the genuine person before me. There was a sense of comfort in how he let his guard down, sharing moments of his life showcased his quirks and genuine nature.

The sunlight filtered through the leaves, casting dappled patterns on the ground and creating a play of shadows. We strolled along the stone pathways, each step accompanied by the soothing sound of our voices and leaves rustling. We approached a small gazebo nestled amidst the vines, and the sight of a wine-tasting station beckoned. The wooden barrels and intricate decor evoked a sense of charm, inviting us to experience the vineyard's offerings. The sound of glasses clinking and laughter drifted towards us.

Aaron and I sat at a quaint table in the vineyard's charming tasting area. Our conversation flowed like a river meandering through the heart of a forest. We discussed everything from our favorite books and movies to our most memorable travel experiences. Each topic unveiled a new layer of our personalities, deepening our connection.

We perused the wine menu, I looked at Aaron and grinned. "So, do you have any preferences when it comes to wine? Reds, whites, or are you more of a rosé person?"

He chuckled, glancing over the menu. "I'm open to trying anything. I have a soft spot for reds, but I'm curious to see what this place offers."

With a nod, I motioned to the server, who approached with a smile. "Good evening! Are you ready to start your wine tastings?" she asked.

"Yes, we would love to," Aaron replied, returning her smile.

I asked, "Could you recommend a selection of wines showcasing the best of what the vineyard has to offer?"

The server nodded, her eyes sparkling. "Of course! Our flight features various signature wines, from light whites to bold reds. It's a great way to experience our range of flavors."

"Sounds perfect," I said, exchanging a glance with Aaron. "We'll go with the flight, please."

The server jotted down our order, and she described each wine on the flight, highlighting its unique characteristics. Aaron and I exchanged intrigued glances throughout her explanation, communicating our anticipation for the tasting experience.

With our order placed, we settled back into our chairs, our conversation picking up seamlessly. We discussed our favorite wine regions and stories of wine-related adventures and even debated the merits of cork versus screw cap closures. Laughter punctuated our conversation, enabling us to move between topics and turning the evening into a mutual journey of discovery. The first glass of wine set before us, we raised our glasses, eyes meeting in a silent toast.

A breeze carried hints of earth and the rich aroma of grapes. The air charged with excitement, the atmosphere alive with the collective enjoyment of those around us. Our day unfolded in a symphony of emotions – curiosity, delight, and a growing sense of connection. We sampled different wines, and our conversations flowed between experiences and future aspirations. The sun continued its slow descent, casting aglow over the landscape and deepening the colors around us.

The afternoon turned to evening. We found ourselves sitting on a vine-covered terrace, glasses of wine in hand. The sky painted itself in shades of orange and pink, casting a dreamlike hue over the scene. Other visitors' soft laughter and murmurs added to the charming ambiance, creating an intimate backdrop for our moments.

The sun descended on the horizon, casting a glow across the vineyard. Aaron and I immersed ourselves in a conversation that felt like a natural continuation of our earlier exchanges.

We spoke about our favorite novels, dissecting characters and plots as if they were old friends we were catching up with. Our enthusiasm for literature turned the conversation into a lively exchange, with recommendations flying back and forth like leaves carried by a breeze.

With a smile, Aaron recounted an amusing travel mishap that had me laughing so hard I could catch my breath. "I can't believe you got stuck in an airport for twelve hours," I teased, shaking my head in mock disbelief.

He grinned, his eyes sparkling with a playful glint. "Believe me, by the end of it, I was contemplating becoming an honorary member of the airport cleaning crew."

Our discussion covered a tapestry of topics – from childhood memories to dreams of future adventures. Our experiences complemented each other.

The sun dipped lower and the air grew cooler, Aaron's jacket draped over my shoulders. His gesture carried a tenderness that tugged at my heartstrings. Turning to him with a grateful smile, the touch of his fingers against my skin sparked a warmth that transcended the fabric. It was a simple act that spoke volumes, reminding us of the connection we were building and our comfort in each other's presence.

In those moments of laughter and the touch of his jacket, I realized this evening was not merely a first date. It was a step towards something more meaningful.

The vineyard's lights twinkled like stars as twilight descended, casting a soft glow illuminating our surroundings. The transition from day to night mirrored the evolution of our connection – a gradual unfolding of deeper layers. We sat lost in conversation, the world around us fading into the background. The rich taste of the wine lingered on my tongue.

A live band began to play nearby, their music weaving through the air and adding a new layer of magic to the evening. Couples danced on a nearby terrace, their movements graceful and synchronized. The music tugged at something within me, a desire to embrace the moment and let go of any reservations.

Aaron's gaze met mine, and without a word, he extended his hand towards me. As our fingers interlocked, a jolt of excitement surged through me. We joined the dancers, swaying to the rhythm of the music beneath the starlit sky.

The world around us blurred as we moved together, our steps matching the cadence of our hearts. The soft rustling of leaves and the distant laughter of other couples merged with the melodies, creating a harmonious symphony. The song ended, and we slowed, catching our breath and sharing a tender smile. The night was filled with endless possibilities and the promise of more moments. We returned to our seats, savoring the remnants of the evening. The stars shone above us, a reminder of moments of beauty and connection to hold onto even amidst life's uncertainties.

In the vineyard's enchanting atmosphere, my emotions swirled like the fragrant notes of our sampled wines. Spending time with Aaron had always been a mixture of comfort and excitement, but this day felt different, deeper. We wandered through the rows of grapevines. His presence beside me stirred a sense of belonging I hadn't experienced before.

His smile lit up his face, and something within me. Each time our eyes met, a silent understanding passed between us. The ease of our conversations and laughter flowed and hinted at a bond that had grown.

With each passing moment, I was drawn to Aaron's presence. His kindness, intelligence, and attentive listening made me feel valued as if my words held immense significance. In his company, I found a sense of safety, an unspoken assurance that I could be myself without fear of judgment.

A subtle shift occurred within me. The butterflies that fluttered in my stomach at the beginning of our date now settled into a more tranquil rhythm. It wasn't solely the beauty of the vineyard or the delightful wine that caused this change – it was the realization that my feelings for Aaron were evolving.

It was the joy of being with him, the thrill of his touch, and the comfort of our connection. It was as if our steps mirrored the journey of my heart, moving from uncertainty to a newfound awareness.

Was I falling in love? The thought lingered in the corners of my mind, a question I dared not answer. Love was complex, a labyrinth of emotions demanding time and understanding. I knew Aaron would become integral to my life, and my feelings for him deepened.

We gazed at the night sky, wrapped in the embrace of the vineyard's tranquility. This date became more than a simple outing. It was a chapter in our story beginning during a challenging investigation. It now found itself in a vineyard, surrounded by laughter, music, and the warmth of newfound emotions.

Epilogue

The air was crisp with the promise of autumn as leaves wore colors of red and gold. The town weathered the storm, emerging stronger, more united, and determined to move forward with transparency and integrity.

The doorbell chimed, and a smile lit up my face as I hurried to answer it. Aaron stood on the threshold, a bouquet in his hand and a familiar twinkle in his eyes.

"Hey, you," I greeted, leaning in for a welcoming kiss. "You're right on time."

"I wouldn't miss it for the world," he replied, his voice a melody resonated with familiarity and affection. "These are for you." He extended the bouquet, a vibrant burst of color mirrored the emotions in our hearts.

Aaron stepped inside, his gaze sweeping across the apartment. He landed on the framed newspaper clipping, taking in the tiny details which became a part of our journey. The story was from the pivotal

Town Hall meeting that united us a year ago and evolved into a deep and meaningful connection.

"I can't believe it's been a year," he mused, his eyes meeting mine with nostalgia and anticipation.

"Time flies," I nodded, guiding him towards the dining area where the table set. "It's been an incredible journey. Tonight, we're celebrating our town's progress and the connection we've built."

"Hey," he said, his eyes lighting up as he looked at me. "Ready to meet up with Holli, Rebeccah, and Samantha for our little journey down memory lane?"

I grinned. "Let's head out."

We walked down the hallway together, descending the stairs of the apartment complex. The sky was painted with golden twilight hues, glowing over the town. My car awaited us in the parking lot, and soon, we were on the road, cruising toward the café where our paths first crossed.

We pulled up to the quaint café. Its familiar red-brick exterior and the glow of lights framing the windows brought memories back. The chance encounter sparked a friendship, leading to discovery and change. The café's windows framed the interior in a warm, welcoming light. Aaron and I entered. We spotted Holli, Rebeccah, and Samantha seated at their usual corner table.

Greeting each other with smiles and hugs, the friends settled in, the familiarity of the café creating an atmosphere of comfort and nostalgia. Chelsea, the waitress who served me the first day, approached the table.

"Welcome back," Chelsea said with a smile. It's been a while. Is this the usual for all of you?"

We exchanged amused glances before nodding in agreement. "The usual" referred to our favorite orders – a strong cappuccino for

Samantha, a blonde latte with two Splenda for Holli, a black coffee for Rebeccah, and a green tea for me. It became a small ritual tying us to this café and its memories.

Chelsea's eyes gleamed as she continued, "You won't believe what's been the talk of the town. A new mystery artist is in our midst, and they've been leaving these incredible, intricate chalk drawings on the sidewalks around town. It's like magic overnight! Nobody knows who they are or when they create these masterpieces."

Her words hung in the air, drawing us into the intrigue of this enigmatic artist's creations. Chelsea's tone had the thrill of discovery. The mere idea of secret chalk drawings painted an alluring picture of an anonymous talent weaving their artistry throughout town.

"People are calling it the 'Chalk Chronicles,'" Chelsea continued, her smile widening. Each drawing tells a different story—whimsical scenes, intricate patterns, and messages of hope. The best part? It's become this sort of treasure hunt. People wake up in the morning and rush out to find the latest creation, sharing photos and speculating about their meaning."

Chelsea went to retrieve our orders, and the conversation flowed. Laughter, anecdotes, and memories were in the air as we caught up on each other's lives. I recounted the latest developments in my journalism career. "The station manager wants me to host all the Town Hall meetings in Centerville," I shared a mix of excitement in my voice. "It's a big responsibility, but I think it's a great opportunity to keep the community engaged."

Samantha leaned in, "That's a significant step forward, Breanna. It shows your work is being recognized and valued. You've come a long way since the first day in this café, right? From uncovering hidden truths to being the voice that bridges the community and its leadership."

This café witnessed countless discussions, supporting our planning sessions and moments of revelation. Amidst the quiet hum of the café, I looked around at my friends, a contemplative air hanging over us. "Isn't it surreal the trial is almost upon us? It's hard to believe after all this time, we're standing on the brink of seeing the culmination of our efforts."

Holli's voice trembled with sentiment. "Every step we've taken in the past year led us to this pivotal juncture. The trial is a chance to witness the real impact of what happened."

Rebeccah acknowledged. "To think we're back in this community, having this conversation – it's a connected circle."

Samantha contributed her perspective. "The array of charges is staggering against Fredrick- bribery, fraud, accessory to arson, and second-degree murder. Like you said, Bre he needs a good lawyer, or he will be an expert at making license plates and find himself there a long time."

The community's response was tangible – town hall meetings were attended more, discussions about civic responsibility became more common, and local businesses began promoting ethical practices. The investigation sparked a cultural shift, encouraging individuals to question the status quo and take a stand against wrongdoing.

A smile spread across my face. The transformation was undeniable, not just within myself but also among those I held dear. Rebeccah's perspective shifted, igniting a fresh sense of purpose radiated from her. Holli's commitment to ethics grew more pronounced, while Samantha's empathy towards those facing challenges deepened. I'd evolved as a community member, learning to embrace traditional values and ethics, long the foundation of our tight-knit town.

Aaron's presence in my life brought about a profound transformation. Our relationship went beyond romance; it's a partnership based on mutual respect and unwavering support. His belief in my abilities boosted my confidence, pushing me to embrace new roles. With him, I've learned to balance my dedication to journalism and community with personal happiness. His constant presence enriches every aspect of my journey, reminding me life's joys are shared. Through him, I've discovered the transformative power of love, inspiring me to dream bigger and make a lasting impact.

Aaron turned and faced me. I noticed he took a deep breath. The twinkle in his eyes matched the soft glow of the café lights, and his voice carried the weight of vulnerability as he began to speak. "Breanna, from the moment we met, you've brought light into my life. You've shown me the power of truth, dedication, and compassion. Through our journey together, I've realized you're not just my partner – my inspiration, my confidante, and the love of my life." His words were a heartfelt decision, and as the depth of his feelings washed over me, my heart raced with emotion. He continued. Anticipation filled the air. "Breanna, I want to spend the rest of my life by your side, facing challenges as a team and celebrating our victories together. Will you marry me?"

With those words, he knelt on one knee, producing a small box with a shimmering ring – a symbol of his commitment and the love grown between us. Time seemed to stand still as the café around us faded into the background, leaving only the echo of his question and the eager beating of our hearts as I responded- "Yes!"

Acknowledgements

Creating a book transcends the solitary act of typing on an author's keyboard. It's a collaborative effort involving numerous individuals, each contributing to the tapestry that brings forth the mesmerizing worlds an author unveils. This book stands as a testament to that collective endeavor. Behind its pages lies a dedicated and talented team fervently weaving together a narrative brimming with strength, transformation, and the enduring bonds of friendship. Thank you to Kendra Coffman, Tiffany Vega, Sara Davil, and my beloved wife Holli. Your unwavering dedication and hard work have brought this story to life in ways I could never have imagined. I am deeply grateful for your support and collaboration. A heartfelt appreciation extends to my cover artist, Sadia Asif. Your creative vision has given this tale its visual essence, breathing life onto its cover and beyond. Yet, paramount among my acknowledgments is to my beloved family. To my wife, Holli, and daughters, Breanna, Rebeccah, and Samantha—you are the heartbeat of my inspiration. Your unwavering love and encouragement have been the guiding light throughout this journey. I cherish you all deeply.

John Russell

Bonus Material InvestigativeSeries Book 3 Kodiak Mysteries

CHAPTER 1

Wrapping up my final tasks at the bustling office. The hum of fluorescent lights and the tap of keyboards echoed. Tomorrow marked the beginning of my vacation escape to Kodiak, a mountain community promising relief from the corporate whirlwind. The demands had been relentless, and this much-needed vacation was like a lifeline.

Exchanging weary smiles and nods with my co-workers as I turned off my computer. Carla, my dedicated assistant, passed by with a knowing look. "Counting down the hours, Rebeccah?" she quipped, her voice tinged with playful sympathy.

I laughed. "More like minutes."

Her eyes crinkled in amusement. "You deserve this break. The team can handle things here."

"Thanks, Carla. I'm leaving things in capable hands." Appreciating her reassurance and the unspoken understanding of our pressures.

Walking to the breakroom, I bumped into Mark, the innovative head of product development. His eyes sparkled with curiosity. "Kodiak, right? Your escape begins tomorrow?"

Replying, relief evident in my tone. "It's time to trade the boardroom for the mountains."

Mark chuckled. "You've earned it. Hey, don't forget to bring back some fresh ideas."

"You understand me too well," I quipped, appreciating his unwavering support for blending business with pleasure.

Heading to my office's exit, I ran into Emily, a vibrant graphic designer. She grinned. "Leaving us for the mountains, Rebeccah? Can't say I blame you."

Laughing. "It's temporary, I promise. I'll be back with a tan and renewed energy."

"I'll hold you to that," Emily winked.

Exiting the office, I noticed a lightness that had been absent for too long. The night air was cool, and the city lights cast a glow. My phone buzzed with a text from Samantha. A simple "Counting down!". The message brought a smile to my lips. Her excitement was infectious.

The night air was cool and refreshing, a welcome departure from the office's air-conditioned confines. The faint scent of nearby food trucks intermingled with the aroma of blooming flowers, created an urban sense.

I found my car. It was a reliable companion seeing me through countless commutes and late nights. Unlocking the doors, I slid into the driver's seat, the leather yielding beneath me.

The car hummed, marking my shift from work to personal time. Dashboard lights illuminated the space, casting a serene glow. Navigating traffic, the city's vitality enveloped me. Music filled the air as I drove past familiar sights, basking in Sunnyville's evening charm. The sun painted the sky in vibrant hues, a mesmerizing sight. Grateful for the respite, I turned towards home, content and at peace.

Walking through the door of my home, I was glad the day's demands had lifted from my shoulders. The inviting warmth of the interior embraced me. I kicked off my shoes near the entryway, and a sense of relief washed over me—the first step to unwinding after a long day.

With a contented sigh, I walked into the living room, my steps echoing against the hardwood floors. The promise of a quiet evening ahead was a comforting thought. In the kitchen, I retrieved a bottle of red wine from the cabinet and poured myself a glass. The rich aroma filled the air. My thoughts turned to the task at hand—packing for my upcoming trip to Kodiak. The suitcase stood in the middle of the room. I opened the suitcase and looked through my dresser for something to put inside.

"I don't want to do this right now. This can wait until morning," I told myself, closing the suitcase and placing it at the foot of my bed.

I entered the living room and settled onto the couch, my body sinking into the plush cushions. Samantha agreed to accompany me on the drive to Kodiak. A familiar warmth spread within me as I thought about the journey ahead.

I reached for my phone and dialed her number. The phone rang, and her voice on the other end carried the comforting cadence of familiarity.

"Hey, Sam," I greeted, a smile forming as her voice greeted me in return.

"Hey, Rebeccah! Are you thrilled about our road trip?" Samantha's enthusiasm was infectious.

www.ingramcontent.com/pod-product-compliance
Lightning Source LLC
Chambersburg PA
CBHW072138300726
48975CB00003B/1120